ROGUE

Nurse Patti Parkin had no intention of falling in love, and certainly had no time at all for Ivor Maynard, known as the Hartlake Heartbreaker. With his reputation, how could she be sure that at last he was serious?

*Books you will enjoy
in our Doctor – Nurse series*

SOUTH ISLAND NURSE by Belinda Dell
OVER THE GREEN MASK by Lisa Cooper
CHATEAU NURSE by Jan Haye
HOSPITAL IN THE MOUNTAINS by Jean Evans
UNCERTAIN SUMMER by Betty Neels
NURSE IN NEW MEXICO by Constance Lea
CARIBBEAN NURSE by Lydia Balmain
DOCTORS IN SHADOW by Sonia Deane
BRIGHT CRYSTALS by Lilian Darcy
NIGHT OF THE MOONFLOWER by Anne Vinton
A BRIDE FOR THE SURGEON by Hazel Fisher
THE DOCTOR'S DECISION by Elizabeth Petty
NURSE RHONA'S ROMANCE by Anne Vinton
THE GAME IS PLAYED by Amii Lorin
DOCTOR IN PLASTER by Lisa Cooper
A MATCH FOR SISTER MAGGY by Betty Neels
HIBISCUS HOSPITAL by Judith Worthy
NURSE AT THE TOP by Marion Collin

ROGUE REGISTRAR

BY

LYNNE COLLINS

MILLS & BOON LIMITED
London · Sydney · Toronto

*First published in Great Britain 1982
by Mills & Boon Limited, 15–16 Brook's Mews,
London W1A 1DR*

© Lynne Collins 1982

*Australian copyright 1982
Philippine copyright 1982*

ISBN 0 263 73771 3

All the characters in this book have no existence outside the imagination of the Author, and have no relation whatsoever to anyone bearing the same name or names. They are not even distantly inspired by any individual known or unknown to the Author, and all the incidents are pure invention.

The text of this publication or any part thereof may not be reproduced or transmitted in any form or by any means, electronic or mechanical, including photocopying, recording, storage in an information retrieval system, or otherwise, without the written permission of the publisher.

This book is sold subject to the condition that it shall not, by way of trade or otherwise, be lent, resold, hired out or otherwise circulated without the prior consent of the publisher in any form of binding or cover other than that in which it is published and without a similar condition including this condition being imposed on the subsequent purchaser.

03/0182

Set in 11 on 12pt Times Roman

*Photoset by Rowland Phototypesetting Ltd
Bury St Edmunds, Suffolk
Made and printed in Great Britain by
Richard Clay (The Chaucer Press) Ltd
Bungay, Suffolk*

CHAPTER ONE

It was one of those mornings.

Currie, Men's Surgical, was always a busy ward. There were always a hundred and one things to do and never enough hands to do them, but by some miracle, and with the driving force of Sister Percival behind them, the ward staff coped with the kind of efficiency that was expected from Hartlake nurses.

Pushing a dressings trolley along the ward, Patti wished that she had at least three pairs of hands. There was little time to notice the brilliant sunshine that streamed through the long ward windows, heralding the summer and lifting the spirits of those patients who were well enough to be thinking of going home. There was even less time to regret that it had been the early hours of the morning before she got to bed after that riotous party. Scrambling through a ground-floor window of the Nunnery, as the Nurses' Home was irreverently known, risking life and limb and Home Sister's wrath, she had not given a thought to the long hours of duty she would have to face. Struggling out of the mists of sleep and yawning through her breakfast, she had reminisced happily about the party with her friends.

Now, working at full stretch because they were short-staffed on the ward, Patti almost wished that she had not gone to the party. But it was not every day that a student nurse celebrated her engagement to a senior doctor, and Daisy was one of her closest friends although they were not in the same set. Daisy was a second year. The single thin blue stripe on Patti's cap betrayed the fact that she was only a first-year nurse.

'Nurse! It's a lovely day, isn't it?'

Patti did not pause. 'Lovely!' she agreed with her swift, warm smile, and hurried on. Mr Bennet was due to be discharged and he was inclined to be talkative and she had very little time to talk to anyone that morning.

'Nurse! I've got a dreadful pain . . .'

Patti halted the trolley and hurried to the patient who called as she reached his bed. He was a young man who had been admitted with classic symptoms of gall-bladder disease for tests and probable surgery. Now, he was lying with knees drawn up, his face ashen and crumpled like a child's with pain.

Sometimes the cry was just a gambit to get a nurse to stop and talk for a few minutes in the course of her busy day. Most nurses learned to recognise the flirts and the grumblers in the early days of training, as well as those patients who faced pain and indignity and sometimes death with cheerful courage.

Patti touched the patient's forehead and found it cold, clammy with sweat. She felt for his pulse. It was slow and sluggish. His body was rigid, fighting pain. She patted his shoulder reassuringly. 'I'll tell Sister . . .' She drew the curtains about the bed and hurried to the office in search of Sister Percival.

Having found her and explained, she went back to the ward. The trolley stood where she had left it.

'Nurse! I'm waiting to get on with the dressings. I wish you wouldn't dawdle when there's so much to be done before doctors' rounds!' Jenefer Neal bustled past, tall and slim and even starchier than usual. She was often sharp with the juniors. It was rumoured by the hospital grapevine that she had been crossed in love. The juniors had decided that she had lost her man to a redhead as she seemed to have a particular down on Patti, whose thick mop of auburn curls provided a very precarious perch for her tiny cap.

Patti helped the staff nurse to change the dressings of several patients. Then she took a patient to theatre. Drowsy with pre-med but still apprehensive, he clung to her hand as she walked beside the trolley and went up with him in the lift. She stayed with him while the anaesthetist put him under in the ante-room with an injection into the vein.

When she returned to the ward, Sister was accompanying Mr Manning, a consultant surgeon, on his round and Jenefer Neal sent her off to busy herself in the sluice. As the most junior of the student nurses on Currie, Patti was general dogsbody. All the most menial and unpopular of chores fell to her lot, but it never occurred to her to complain. Long hours, hard work, sometimes difficult patients, frequently bossy seniors and constantly aching legs and feet were just minor drawbacks when one loved nursing.

Other girls in her set might decide that the job was not for them and give it up. Some might fall in love and get married before they completed the three-year course of training. Patti knew that the job was for her and she had no intention of falling in love. Never again. Once had proved to be more than enough heartache. But that was something she had come to Hartlake to forget, and she was much too busy to dwell on it now as she sluiced and sterilised bedpans.

She was very happy on Currie. She had liked Fleming, Men's Medical, where she had worked with Daisy and observed the progress of her romance with Gavin Fletcher with a great deal of satisfaction. But a surgical ward really satisfied her need to be busy, to have no time to think about the past or the might-have-been.

On Currie, there was only time to think about the needs of the patients and attend to them. They had their hands full with the preparation of patients for theatre, half-hourly observations on newly postoperative patients, the need to 'special' the very ill and the routine nursing of the convalescent as well as coping with frequent emergency admissions.

On Currie, there was a constant to and fro of doctors and medical students, anaesthetists and pathologists, lab technicians and dieticians and physiotherapists and a variety of ancillary hospital staff as well as anxious relatives and friends. The ward telephone seemed never to be silent, its shrill tone blending with the trundle of trolleys, the clatter of instruments and the 'bleep' of personal radios worn by the medical staff.

And, of course, there were always 'rounds'. Drugs, pulse and temps, b.p's, fluid charts, dressings, bedpans and bedmaking, blanket baths and back rubs, meals and hot drinks . . . all the many chores that made up a nurse's busy day. Senior Sister Tutor in the early days at the Preliminary Training School had stressed the need for such chores to be carried out with a smile and a cheerful word for the benefit of the patients. Patti liked people and she had a warm heart and a fund of sympathy for the sick and elderly. She found it easy to smile, to find the right words to cheer and reassure, to get on with the routine work with the philosophical acceptance that someone had to do it.

Some of her set grumbled that they were little more than wardmaids. Patti argued that their contribution left the senior nurses free to get on with the real business of nursing. In time, they would qualify as senior nurses. In the meantime, sluicing bedpans and changing dirty linen and scurrying about the wards at the bidding of autocrats like Jenefer Neal was just part and parcel of the job they had chosen to do.

Several juniors claimed that they had known since childhood that they wanted to nurse. Patti had never thought of nursing. She had set her heart on marriage, home and children from the first moment of meeting Steve. All her friends had been career girls and her views had been mocked as old-fashioned. But she had been quite sure that it would be sufficiently satisfying for her to be a good wife and mother.

But Steve had married someone else and Patti had resigned herself to being a career girl, after all. What better career than nursing, with its variety of interest and guaranteed job satisfaction? More to the point, perhaps, training at a teaching hospital in

London would put a great many miles between herself and possible encounters with Steve and his lovely wife.

Hartlake was very selective. Because of its long traditions and high standards, it took only the best. So Patti had been particularly pleased to be accepted for its training school by the hospital whose nurses were known and valued throughout the world. She did not expect to forget Steve. That was not possible. But nursing was helping her to live with her heartache.

The first essential for a nurse was to forget her own concerns when she came on to the ward. She might have any number of problems or anxieties. She might be on top of the world or in the depths of despair according to the progress of her love life. But she must forget it all as she put on the crisp white apron that was a nurse's symbol of being on duty, pinned her cap securely in place and joined the rest of her shift for Report.

On a ward like Currie, with its daily demands and dramas, its many seriously ill patients and the need to accept that some would not survive surgery, it was not so difficult for Patti to forget her own affairs. At times, the ache of missing Steve faded into complete insignificance as she comforted a young woman who had just lost her husband, or made tea for anxious parents who awaited the result of an operation on a dangerously ill son, or noted the strain in the eyes of relatives resigned to the worst as they came into the ward at visiting time.

It was not a happy ward; too many of the patients were very ill, some with incurable cancers. But

Sister Percival did her best to make it as cheerful as possible for patients and staff. She was a grey-haired dumpling whose looks and manner belied her efficiency and long experience. Beaming and bustling about the ward like a mother-hen with too many chicks, she was a great favourite with the patients. She was kindly and gentle and her nurses held her in respect and affection. They would work till they dropped rather than disappoint her obvious faith in their stamina and good cheer in the face of all odds. She had never been known to scold or to lose her temper and she ran a very busy and demanding ward with the seeming minimum of effort.

She was not in the least like the legendary Sister Booth, a dragon of a ward sister who was now retired but still remembered by those who had suffered from her iron discipline and sharp tongue. Patti hoped to be a ward sister one day and she was determined to be loved like Sister Percival and not disliked and feared like Sister Booth.

Sister Percival put her head round the door of the sluice just as Patti finished the last of the bedpans.

'There you are, Nurse. I want you to run down for Mr Manzi's X-rays. Be as quick as you can. They should have been in his folder before Mr Manning arrived for his round. As soon as you get back you can go for your break.'

'Yes, Sister. Thank you, Sister.'

Ann Percival looked after her newest junior as she hurried along the corridor and pushed through the swing doors. She had great hopes for the girl, who was one of the best nurses to emerge from the Preliminary Training School for some time. It would be sad if she left to marry as so many of them did, but that pretty face and warm heart was not likely to be overlooked in a place where romance was so rife. Matron might frown on flirtation among the staff, but it went on—right under her nose in many cases. Young doctors were susceptible and young nurses fell in love very easily.

Nurse Parkin was an attractive girl, with those unmistakable auburn curls and the sparkle in her smiling green eyes. That warm and vivacious prettiness combined with a lively sense of mischief and the genuine interest and friendliness of manner made her a favourite with almost everyone, and many of the patients visibly perked up when she came on duty.

As did many of the medical staff, thought Ann Percival dryly. Long hours and concentrated study on the wards or in theatres or clinics meant that medical students and recently-qualified housemen needed to relax at the end of a long day. They naturally chose to unwind in the company of a pretty girl whenever opportunity offered, and there were plenty of opportunities for flirtation in a big teaching hospital. Junior nurses, some of them more interested in men than medicine, were easily impressed by the air of confidence and a certain glamour that young doctors seemed to don with their white coats.

Sister of a busy ward for several years, Ann Percival knew all the dangers of throwing young people together in the kind of environment that encouraged them to cast caution to the winds when they were free of the demands and discipline of the wards. Nursing was hard work, and the juniors were expected to enjoy a full social life when the long hours of study allowed.

Nurse Parkin was slightly older than the average student nurse in the first year of training. She seemed a sensible, level-headed girl, and all her reports indicated that she would make a very good nurse. She seemed to have plenty of friends, but there did not appear to be any man of particular importance in her life at the moment. She might just prove to be one of those dedicated girls who regarded medicine as a much more rewarding career than marriage . . .

No one could find the missing X-rays. One of the radiographers insisted that they had been sent up to Currie that morning and was inclined to resent the implication of inefficiency. Patti hastily soothed the ruffled feathers and turned away.

Making her way back to the ward, hurrying through the labyrinth of corridors that linked the various departments and which she had found so confusing in her early days at Hartlake, Patti was hailed by a friend.

Joanne Laidlaw was a one-time student nurse who had been unable to conquer a tendency to sicken at the sight of blood. Disappointed in her original ambition and wanting very much to be involved in hospital work, she was now training as a physiotherapist. She was Daisy's friend and flatmate and she had been the life and soul of the party on the previous evening. She did not even look heavy-eyed that morning, Patti noted enviously.

'I don't suppose you even went to bed, but you

look as if you've had twelve hours of beauty sleep! How do you do it?'

Joanne laughed. 'It was a super party, wasn't it? But I shall miss Daisy dreadfully. We've had a lot of good times. Patti, I've been thinking. Would you like to share the flat with me when Daisy moves out? I can't possibly afford to run it on my own and there isn't anyone I'd rather share with than you.'

Patti had been half-expecting the invitation. In fact, she had more or less sown the seed when she first heard about Daisy's wedding plans.

Matron liked her first-year nurses to live in unless they had family homes within easy reach of the hospital. Patti shared a flat with three other girls in the modern Nurses' Home. It was comfortable and convenient and cheap, and she got on well with her flatmates. But there were advantages to moving in with Joanne. Home Sister Vernon was a sweetie who kept a motherly eye on her charges. Patti felt that she had outgrown that kind of protective supervision. She was not a dewy-eyed innocent of eighteen, straight from school. She would welcome the freedom of being able to come and go at whatever hour of the day or night she chose. It was really rather undignified to be crawling through windows at dead of night like a naughty schoolgirl, after all. She did not have very much in common with her youthful flatmates and she had naturally gravitated towards friendship with Daisy and Joanne, both nearer her age. It would be rather fun to share with Joanne, who had a host of friends and loved parties. It would be nice to entertain her own friends beneath her own roof, too.

'I shall need Matron's permission, but I don't see why she should refuse. I'm quite old enough to look after myself. Thanks, Jo, I'd like it very much,' she said. She went on her way, pleased.

Back on the ward, the X-rays were found after a frantic search, inadvertently tucked into another patient's file. A little flustered because it had been her mistake, although she did not mean to admit it, Jenefer Neal sent Patti to Sister with the folder.

Mr Manning and his students were grouped about a patient's bed. Sister always accompanied the consultants on their rounds and another staff nurse was in charge of the trolley with its neat array of files. Trying to make herself invisible and ignoring the looks and smiles of the students, Patti slipped the X-ray folder into the staff nurse's hand and turned away.

She caught the eye of the patient in the next bed, visibly distressed. She went to him. 'What's the matter, Mr Willis? Aren't you comfortable?'

He clutched a little blindly at her arm, blinking away tears. 'He says me leg's got to come off, Nurse.' He jerked his head in the direction of the tall consultant. 'I don't think I can take that somehow. I've always been a bit of a coward.'

'I'm sure that isn't true,' Patti said gently, thinking how bravely he had borne the pain of a gangrenous condition of the big toe.

'I was expecting the foot. I mean, he warned me of that when I come in. I'd prepared meself for that. But not the leg. That's a bit of a stunner,' he said bleakly.

'Of course it's a shock—and I'm sure Mr Manning is most upset about it. But if it's your leg or your life then there isn't any choice, is there?' She smiled at him warmly, with real understanding and compassion. 'We'll see you through it, Mr Willis . . . and you'll be chasing the nurses in no time at all with your new leg, believe me!'

He smiled wanly. At seventy-three, he was past chasing the girls. But she was a nice little girl and she meant well and somehow nothing seemed quite so bad when she smiled her lovely smile and patted his hand. It had been a shock, but the doctors knew what they were doing and he had a lot of faith in the Hartlake. It had seen his family through some bad times and never failed them yet, after all.

Patti was genuinely concerned. She knew he was an uncomplaining little man and many of the patients were so awed by the consultant's manner that they did not question anything he said. Failure to react in any way to the announcement might have led the consultant to assume that the patient had been prepared by Sister or the houseman for the news. In fact, shock and dismay had probably kept the old man silent.

She sought out Jenefer Neal, troubled. 'Mr Willis is very upset, Staff. He's had such bad news about his leg and he seems to be fretting over it. It was a shock to him, apparently. Do you think Mr Lewis would prescribe a sedative for him?'

'You first years get more uppity every day!' Jenefer was busy and irritable. 'I expect Sister knows his state of mind and she'll speak to the houseman about him if she thinks it necessary. You seem to believe that you're God's gift to nursing! We managed very well on this ward before you came to it, you know!'

'Yes, of course, Staff. Sorry . . .'

Meekly, Patti backed away and returned to her work, wondering why she seemed to alienate the staff nurse without even trying and if it was true that her senior had been jilted for a girl with similar colouring to her own. It might explain that unfounded dislike and hostility.

She was thankful that she did not resent every fair-haired girl she met just because Steve had fallen headlong in love with her blonde cousin and married her. Some of her best friends at Hartlake were blondes, she thought with wry amusement.

Loving seemed responsible for more heartache than happiness. It was not surprising that she was determined to avoid it in future. She was older than most girls who came into nursing, and she often said that the five years between eighteen and twenty-three were a lifetime of experience. Some of it was very useful at times.

Certainly she was not a green girl, straight from school like some of her set, easily flattered or unduly impressed by flirtatious overtures from students or housemen. She did not flirt and would not encourage any of her admirers to expect more than a friendly relationship. She had come to Hartlake to nurse and not to be a doctor's delight, she would declare with a smile that took the sting from the words. She did not add, as she might have done, that she had no heart for any man but Steve.

He was married, now. But five years of loving could not be wiped out, forgotten. She might not be left with any of her youthful dreams of happiness but she could not stop loving him. She was a one-man woman.

It seemed that her future lay in nursing and, being Patti, she had made up her mind to be a good nurse. She knew that she would never marry, after all. Being Patti, she brought the same kind of single-minded purpose to nursing as she had to loving.

As she went along the corridor to the juniors' room for her break, a tall and very attractive man emerged from one of the side wards.

Ivor Maynard was known as the Hartlake Heart-breaker and Patti had no time at all for his kind. Much too handsome, much too sure of himself, his reputation for careless and uncaring affairs with a variety of much too trusting junior nurses far outweighed his qualities as a clever and caring surgeon, in her view.

He was junior registrar to Oliver Manning, the consultant who had recently married a ward sister and provoked a rush of romantic fancies among all the would-be doctor's wives at Hartlake. Eligible and good-looking bachelors like Ivor Maynard had come in for a great deal of attention.

Patti's heart had never fluttered or her pulses quickened for a glance from those dark-blue eyes or one of his engaging smiles. She admitted that he was very attractive, with his crisply curling black hair, his lean features and the deep-set eyes that crinkled when he smiled, and she could appreciate the impact of his good looks and his undeniable charm on an impressionable junior. But she despised his reputed readiness to take advantage of innocence and inexperience. It seemed that he had broken too many hearts during his time at Hartlake.

The grapevine might not be a very reliable source of information, and perhaps his exploits had been much exaggerated, but there was no smoke without fire. Patti did not really doubt that he was the kind of sensual, rakish man who took what he wanted with little thought for the consequences. It was stamped all over him.

Not the kind of man she would wish to include among her friends, she felt . . .

CHAPTER TWO

'Nurse! I want you!'

Without ceremony, she was taken by the arm and urged into the small room. Patti might have resented his peremptory manner and that rather painful grip on her arm if she had not realised the urgency in his deep voice and seen the condition of the patient.

Mr Fielding was a big man who had worked in the docks for many years. He had undergone a major stomach operation on the previous day. Now, confused by pain-killing drugs, he had tried to get out of bed and pulled out a drainage tube and dislodged his drip in doing so.

Ivor needed assistance and there was no time to wait until a more experienced nurse came along the corridor. One glance had told him that the girl was a first year. He needed another pair of hands and it really did not matter if they belonged to a student nurse or a ward sister. She had only to follow his instructions.

Patti managed to do so without mishap and felt that she acquitted herself fairly well at short notice. Ivor Maynard said nothing to her beyond telling her what he wanted. His manner was wholly impersonal, intent on what he was doing.

By the time Jenefer Neal arrived on the scene, having been alerted by a passing third year, the drip had been re-connected and the tube was in the process of being firmly strapped back into place. The patient had quietened after uttering a stream of abuse that had brought a hint of colour to Patti's cheeks.

'Very well, Nurse. I'll take over,' Jenefer said briskly, rather cool. But her eyes were warm as they rested on Ivor Maynard who did not look up as Patti stepped back to allow the staff nurse to take her place. 'Change that apron before you do anything else!'

'Yes, Staff. Thank you, Staff.' The response was automatic. So was obedience, one of the first things that a nurse had to learn. Patti hurried out of the room and went to change into a clean apron.

Ivor glanced after the trim figure in the blue check dress with its puffed sleeves and neat little collar and the matching belt of the first-year nurse. Hartlake had not adopted the national uniform for its nurses and the distinctive dresses were a precious part of its long tradition. Idly, he wondered how she achieved the seemingly impossible of keeping that ridiculous little cap in place. He thought he would recognise those burnished copper curls the next time he saw them, cap or no cap.

She was a very pretty girl. He had noticed her on the ward, of course. She had never appeared to notice him. That might be discretion or it might be lack of interest. Junior nurses usually went out of their way to attract his attention and it amused him to gratify them with a little meaningless flattery and flirtation. Sometimes he took it further, risking

Matron's displeasure and a reprimand from the higher authorities. But, as a rule, it was usually the nurse who was hauled before Matron for a warning if she was foolish enough to parade her friendship with a member of the medical staff.

'Nurse Parkin is very new to nursing,' Jenefer said dismissively, slapping scissors into his waiting hand. 'I'm afraid she can't have been of much use to you. Why on earth didn't you send her to find me or one of the other seniors?'

'She did very well,' Ivor commended lightly. 'She's intelligent and she anticipates. She should make an excellent theatre nurse one day.'

'If she lasts the course.' Jenefer was tart. 'But that kind of girl only comes into nursing to find a husband, I'm afraid.'

Ivor smiled. 'Popular, is she?' The staff nurse was jealous and it showed. He had only taken her out two or three times but, like too many girls, she was already beginning to feel that she had a prior claim to his attention and interest.

'Too popular! That type is a nuisance on a busy ward, frankly. The students are always finding trivial excuses to haunt the ward and they waste her time and their own. And she gossips with the patients and takes far too long over the simplest job. Sister Percival is really much too easy-going with the juniors.'

Ivor nodded absently. He checked the steady flow of the drip and turned towards the door. 'He should do now. But I'd like a closer eye kept on him—and sides on the bed to keep him from getting out again. See to it, will you, Staff?' He was deliberately formal.

'Yes, of course, Mr Maynard.'

She was brisk, efficient, the well-trained nurse. Ivor remembered the abandon with which she had clung to him at their last encounter and his surprise that the iceberg of the ward should be capable of so much passion. Instinctively wary of that kind of intensity, he was in no hurry to repeat the experience.

The "bleep" in his pocket took him from the room and along the corridor to the nearest telephone. He was talking into it when the pretty redhead came out of the room where the juniors kept their capes and clean aprons. She glanced at him. Ivor winked. She began to walk towards the swing doors of the main ward. Even with his admiring eyes on her, she did not show any sign of self-consciousness. He liked her confidence. He fancied that he could span that slender waist with his hands with room to spare. He saw that her eyes were green, unusual and striking, fringed by thick dark lashes.

'I'll be right down . . .' he said into the telephone and replaced the receiver as she reached him. He smiled at her and fell into step beside her. 'Nurse Parkin, isn't it?' he said lightly, undeterred by the etiquette that decreed that senior doctors did not engage junior nurses in private conversation on the wards.

Patti looked at him warily, suspicious of the gleam in his dark eyes. She was not pleased to have attracted his apparently fickle interest. She preferred the impersonality of doctor and nurse. 'Yes.' Her tone was not encouraging.

'Fairly new to the ward, aren't you? And to nursing. I'm afraid I threw you in at the deep end. But it's a good way to learn. Sink or swim. You did very well.'

'It wasn't very sensible,' Patti told him bluntly, ignoring the etiquette which decreed that junior nurses did not criticise senior doctors. 'I might have done all the wrong things.'

His smile deepened. 'But you didn't. You coped. We need more nurses like you.' His eyes crinkled at the corners in the way that had disarmed and charmed a great many women. 'If only to brighten a busy doctor's day with that pretty face.'

Patti's chin went up and impatience sparked in her eyes. 'I didn't come to Hartlake to brighten the day for you or any other doctor,' she said coolly. 'I'm interested in the patients and their welfare and nothing else. Don't waste your time or mine with compliments.' It was a put-down that should leave him in no doubt of her lack of interest. She pushed through the swing doors and into the ward.

Ivor felt dismissed. It was a novel experience. Girls usually responded just as he wished to a smile, a word, a little attention. But there had not been the least flicker of response in those lovely eyes. He fancied that they had seen right into the heart of him and disliked what they found. His interest quickened.

She was not only a very pretty girl. She was mature and confident and not easily swayed by the charm that had won him any woman he wanted in the past.

It was a challenge to a man like Ivor. But registrars were very busy men. He could not spend the rest of the morning on Currie within sight and sound of a nurse whose first name he did not even know. He was due in Out-Patients, overdue, in fact, he reminded himself and turned towards the lift.

Making his way to that busy department, with its variety of clinics and the orderly rows of patient people, Ivor mentally reviewed the rest of his day. Clinic would take up what was left of the morning. A hurried lunch would be followed by conference with Oliver Manning and the other members of his team before work began on the very long list in Theatres. Finally, he would make another round of the wards to check the condition of post-operative patients and discuss their care and treatment with the ward staff.

It promised to be such a hectic day that he would have no time to think about a copper-haired nurse. She would probably come to mind when he was off duty and able to relax. There were plenty of attractive and amenable girls in his life. But the pretty Nurse Parkin tugged very strongly at his interest. She was too attractive and too feminine to be as indifferent to a man's interest as she seemed. He had noticed that she did not wear a wedding ring, the only jewellery that a nurse on duty was allowed to wear. He did not suspect the existence of an engagement ring on a chain about her neck. In his experience, girls were always swift to inform him and the world at large if they were engaged.

Perhaps she was wary of him because of his reputation. Ivor knew his nickname, but felt it was rather unfair of the grapevine to imply that he set out deliberately to break hearts. It was not his fault that impressionable girls fell too easily in love and built hopes and dreams of happy ever after on the flimsy foundation of his fleeting interest. He did not encourage any girl to love him or to suppose that he would marry her. In fact, it was his policy to make it clear at the beginning of an affair that he was not a marrying man. It baffled him that it did not seem to deter the girls from going out with him—or from falling in love, unfortunately. Ivor found it annoying to have to end a relationship because a girl's feeling for him became too intense. He had lost several girl-friends that way.

He had no desire to marry. He did not think he was the type to settle down with one woman for any length of time. He was good at his job and he was ambitious and he had every hope of gaining a consultancy in due course. He needed all his energy and enthusiasm for his work and he simply could not afford to commit himself to the kind of loving that led to marriage. He liked the company of women. A sensual man, he took what came his way and enjoyed it. But he was neither promiscuous nor irresponsible and he would welcome a more lasting relationship that did not make too many demands on him. He wished he could meet a woman who felt the same way . . .

Patti did not mean to give Ivor Maynard another thought as she went into the ward. She would probably have forgotten their encounter if it had not been blown up out of all proportion by Jenefer Neal.

The staff nurse followed her into the ward, seething. Busy in the stock-room, she had recognised the voices without being near enough to make out the words. But, knowing Ivor Maynard, she did not doubt that he had been trying to persuade the junior nurse to meet him off the ward.

Everything about Patti Parkin irritated Jenefer. Her name, the cool confidence, the lively personality, the bright hair and dancing green eyes, the popularity she enjoyed and the admiration she evoked among the patients as well as the male members of the staff. Grudgingly, she admitted that the girl's work was good and that she seemed to care about the patients and promised to be a good and responsible nurse. But she did not appear to take anything seriously. Jenefer took most things very seriously indeed and she could not forgive such a light-hearted attitude. Nor did she mean to tolerate open breaches of hospital etiquette!

'Nurse Parkin!'

Patti turned obediently. 'Yes, Staff?'

'How many times do I have to tell you about that kind of thing?' Jenefer demanded, eyes blazing with hostility.

Patti was taken aback, puzzled. 'What kind of thing? I don't know what you mean.'

'Of course you do! Don't play the injured innocent! You're always hanging about the corridor to catch anything in a white coat that comes along! I've warned you about chatting up the doctors and you'll find yourself on Matron's Report if you persist in flouting the rules. Girls like you make me sick. I don't know why you bother to pretend that you're interested in nursing when it's obvious that you're only interested in meeting men!'

Patti was very angry, outwardly calm. She met the accusing eyes of the staff nurse and said quietly, reasonably: 'I talk to anyone who likes to talk to me, Staff. Patients, relatives, doctors, hospital porters . . . anyone. I have a friendly nature.'

'You're a flirt!'

Patti raised an eyebrow. 'Oh, come on. A few minutes of conversation with a man doesn't make me a flirt, you know.'

'You're man-mad!' Jenefer snapped coldly. 'I don't care what you do off duty. That's your business. But I do care how you behave when you're wearing that uniform. We can do without your kind at Hartlake, my girl!'

Patti turned on her heel and walked away, committing the cardinal sin of not waiting to be dismissed by her senior.

'Nurse! Come back here!'

Patti ignored the furious words. She saw no reason why she should allow herself to be slanged by an almost hysterical staff nurse in full view of the watching and wondering patients. They might not be able to hear the exchange but they could certainly see that Jenefer Neal was in a towering temper.

'Getting at you again, is she, gel?' Old Mr Bruce oozed sympathy as she paused by his bed to retrieve the newspaper that had slid to the floor. 'That one don't like anyone much, do she?'

Patti smiled at him. 'Juniors are always doing daft things,' she said lightly. 'It's her job to straighten us out.'

She plumped his pillows and settled him more comfortably, listening with half an ear as he talked about the daughter who was coming to see him that afternoon. She knew that Jenefer Neal had stalked off in search of Sister and guessed she would shortly be summoned to the office. She told herself firmly that her conscience was clear, but she could not help feeling anxious.

The staff nurse had disliked her from the first day that she set foot on Currie. Patti liked to be on good terms with everyone and it bothered her that Jenefer Neal was determined to criticise her work and her behaviour no matter what she did. No doubt Sister Percival was quite capable of judging for herself, but much of the responsibility for training the juniors had to be delegated to her senior staff nurse. Her report on Patti's work was bound to be influenced by what she heard from Jenefer Neal and Patti was very anxious not to get a bad report on this ward. She sighed.

'Never mind, gel. They can't shoot you,' Mr Bruce comforted, patting her hand. 'It's a crying shame the way they work you nurses—and nag you up hill and down dale into the bargain!'

'Nurse Parkin! Sister wants to see you in her office as soon as possible!'

The message was thrown at her in passing by a scurrying second-year who did not even have time to send her a commiserating smile.

Patti went. A nurse ignored that kind of summons at her peril, she thought ruefully. She knocked lightly on the open office door and went in to face her fate.

Sister Percival was busy with some of the routine paperwork that took up so much of her day. She looked up, smiled. Patti visibly relaxed.

'Oh, Nurse. I understand that you missed your break,' she said in her warm, kindly manner. 'Nurse Neal tells me that you were helping Mr Maynard with a patient in the temporary absence of a senior nurse.'

'Yes, Sister.'

'I expect you gained from the experience. Mr Maynard is one of our best doctors. For that reason, I'm inclined to forgive the fatal effect of his charm on too many of my nurses.' Her eyes twinkled. 'I don't forgive my nurses so easily if their work or behaviour suffers as a result. I might understand but I won't condone.' Her tone was light, very gentle, but the words held an unmistakable warning. 'You must have a break, Nurse,' she went on, concerned. 'You may take it now.'

'Yes, Sister. Thank you, Sister.' Patti turned towards the door.

Sister Percival's soft voice checked her. 'You will apologise to Nurse Neal, of course. You may have felt justified, but apparently you undermined her authority before the patients. It mustn't happen again.'

'No, Sister. I'm sorry, Sister,' Patti said meekly and escaped. She made herself coffee in the juniors' room, warming to the understanding woman who had obviously listened to what Jenefer Neal had to say and made up her own mind. She did not care what the staff nurse thought. She cared very much for Sister Percival's good opinion.

Later, she sought the staff nurse and made her apology. It was received with tight-lipped frigidity.

Patti was rushed off her feet for the rest of the day. They were short-staffed, it was true. Five patients were listed for Theatres and they had three emergency admissions that afternoon. But she knew that Jenefer Neal was deliberately piling the work on her. She sorted and tidied linen, checked stock, scrubbed out the sluice, sterilised instruments, hurried with messages or forms to various wards and hospital departments, did teas, helped with rounds and was, as usual, general dogsbody.

She did not mind. But the patients missed her brief, friendly chats as she went about her work on the ward.

For Patti was a talker when patients needed cheering or stirring to greater efforts or just the comfort of her bright voice filtering through a drug-induced drowsiness. She was a good listener, too. The kind of nurse who was normally never too busy to talk to a patient even when she had several things to do. She felt that there were times when it was impossible to ignore the need for comfort or reassurance, or just a friendly word to make someone feel like a person and not just another name on a medical chart.

But with Jenefer Neal's cold eye upon her and the feeling that Sister was watching very closely for the least sign that she was neglecting her work, Patti just did as she was bid and waited for the dust to settle.

She was very tired by the end of the long day, looking forward to a quiet evening and an early night. She was just going off duty when Ivor Maynard came back to the ward for his final round of the day. He was talking to Marian Foster, a third-year nurse, when Patti came out of the juniors' room, drawing her outdoor cape about her shoulders in readiness for the short walk along the High Street.

Patti glanced at the couple incuriously and then felt a prickle of irritation as she saw that Marian's coquettish attitude offered him a great deal of encouragement. She did not approve of the readiness of her sex to appreciate his good looks, his smiling charm. Any man would become insufferably conceited in the face of so much attention.

She hurried along the corridor, seeing no reason to acknowledge him. He was much too familiar a figure on the ward.

As she reached them, he turned with a swift, warm smile that might have impressed a more susceptible girl. 'Goodnight . . .' he said lightly.

Patti smiled back at him without even thinking about it and hurried on, quite unaware that her small face had been illumined to beauty in that brief moment. It seemed to Ivor, who was not a fanciful man, that the sun suddenly shone in that windowless corridor between wards.

When Patti reached the Nurses' Home, she found that her flatmates had already settled down to their studies. She sank into a chair and kicked off her black brogues and could not even summon the energy to fill the kettle.

'I'm dead,' she declared. 'What a day! I'm only fit to crawl into bed.'

Jacqui looked up from her book with a smile. She

was a slender, pretty girl with long fair hair that she knotted on the nape of her neck when on duty. 'If someone rang with an invite to a party you'd be dressed and raring to go within half an hour!' she declared, knowing her friend.

'Not tonight,' Patti said firmly. 'No more parties for me! I just haven't the stamina to be up half the night and run round in circles for bad-tempered staff nurses all day.'

Phyllida lifted her dark head from the anatomy textbook she was studying. 'Feeling your age?' she teased.

'Probably.' Patti grinned. 'I wish some kind friend would revive me with a cup of tea,' she added hopefully.

Kate rose from the book-strewn table, always glad of an excuse to abandon her studies. She reached for the kettle. 'That boy with the stab wound ended up on Currie, didn't he? How is he? I was in A and E when he came in.' She pushed a wing of heavy blonde hair from her face. Cut short in the latest fashion, it had a mind of its own and flopped forward to annoy her instead of staying in place as it should.

'He'll do, apparently.' Patti used the traditional term for patients who were expected to make a full recovery. 'He'd lost a lot of blood but it was a clean cut and missed any vital organs. Was it a fight, do you know?'

'Outside the Kingfisher, I believe. More of a scuffle than a proper fight. There were a lot of half-drunk lads milling about the place—and the police, of course. Never a dull moment on A and E,' she said with obvious satisfaction.

'There aren't many on Currie,' Patti told her dryly—and wondered why it leaped to her mind that the ward was enlivened by the presence of good-looking registrars as well as the usual daily activities that kept them all so busy.

CHAPTER THREE

THE Kingfisher was a popular haunt for the locals as well as the staff of the famous hospital just across the road. The licensee, Jim Carver, had been in Currie Ward earlier that year, having collapsed in the bar to provide a classic textbook case of peritonitis for the benefit of the medical students he was serving at the time.

The following evening, Patti made her way through the crush in the lounge bar, looking for Joanne. Her friend had telephoned the Nurses' Home to invite her for a drink in the pub so that they could discuss all the arrangements for sharing the flat after Daisy's wedding next month.

It had been another busy day on Currie and London seemed to be basking in a mini heat-wave. Tired and hot and jaded, Patti had suggested that they should make it another evening. Jo had been very persuasive. She needn't change. She had only to cross the road. It needn't be a late night. So Patti had agreed that it was rather tame to spend the evening with her books and have an early night.

She had showered and put on a cream linen dress and run a brush through her curls. She looked cool and pretty, attracting attention and greetings from several people in the pub. She smiled, nodded, paused to speak to Marian Foster, the third year on Currie. A daring medical student rumpled her bright curls. Another, even more daring, put an arm about her waist and planted a beery kiss on her cheek.

Patti laughed, wriggled away and looked about her for Jo. She felt a momentary dismay as she saw her friend in a corner with John Seymour, the houseman who was her most constant boy-friend, and another couple. Jo had led her to believe that she would be on her own.

Jo saw her, waved.

Patti went to join the group. She liked John and hoped that he and Joanne would make a match of it eventually. Like many newly qualified doctors, he could not afford to think of marriage yet, and Jo was inclined to be flirtatious, rather fickle. She was a beautiful girl with her chestnut curls and sapphire eyes and the golden smile that captivated so many men.

Patti slid into the seat beside her friend. 'Hi . . .'

Joanne welcomed her warmly. 'I'm glad you decided to come.'

'Who needs sleep?' Patti quipped, a little dry. She was puzzled by Jo's insistence that she should join what had turned out to be a party. She did not think that there would be much opportunity to discuss flat-sharing in the hubbub of the Kingfisher.

She felt her hackles rise as she saw Ivor Maynard approaching their corner with a tray of drinks. She had not seen him standing at the bar. As their eyes met, he smiled at her with warmth and an unmistakable gleam of satisfaction and Patti realised that she had been lured to the pub that evening at his instigation.

She was not flattered. She was not at all interested in him. She had seen him about the ward during the day and taken pains to avoid him as much as possible. She had snubbed him very plainly on the previous day. So why should he pursue someone with whom he had barely exchanged two words? She forgot that she had smiled with spontaneous, unthinking friendliness when he stood talking to Marian, the night before. She was unaware of the impact of that enchanting smile on a man who had known and carelessly loved any number of women, but could not chase a copper-headed junior nurse from his thoughts.

'You know Ivor, don't you . . . ?' Jo's introduction was so airy as to be non-existent. She looked just a little conscious, realising that Patti was not too pleased to discover that the rakish registrar was one of the party.

'No,' Patti said bluntly, uncompromising.

Jo had turned back to John, not listening. Ivor smiled, undismayed by the snub. 'Then you should,' he said lightly. He handed round the drinks and placed a glass in front of Patti. 'Martini and lemonade. Jo tells me that's your tipple.'

Patti resisted the temptation to push it back to him. That would be childish. But she was annoyed at being forced to accept a drink from a stranger she did not really want to know. 'Thanks,' she said, short, ungracious.

Ivor and Joanne exchanged brief glances. Her slim shoulders lifted in the slightest of shrugs as if to deny all responsibility for her friend's attitude.

He smiled at her, reassuring, and sat down beside

the stiffly resisting Patti. He found it refreshing that she was not prepared even to meet him halfway. She was certainly different from most of the girls who had caught his fancy in the past.

'I hoped we would meet without Sister or Nurse Neal breathing down your neck,' he said lightly. 'Dame Fortune seems to be on my side for once.'

Patti was not impressed by the twinkle in his dark eyes. She wondered how he had persuaded Jo to make that telephone call. Dame Fortune, indeed! 'You and Dame Fortune are both wasting your time,' she said lightly, discouraging any hopes he might have where she was concerned. 'I'm not interested in anything you have to offer.'

He raised an amused eyebrow. 'You don't know what I'm offering, girl,' he drawled.

'I think I do,' she retorted, very dry.

Ivor laughed, reached for his beer. He had felt very tempted to know more of Nurse Parkin, away from the restrictive atmosphere and influences of the ward. Chance had played into his hands . . . Crossing Main Hall on his way to make a final tour of the wards that evening, he had paused for a word with Jimmy, Head Porter, who had been at Hartlake for over thirty years and was something of an institution.

Everyone knew Jimmy. He prided himself on knowing everyone at Hartlake by name or sight. A big man with a bubbling sense of humour, blessed with a warm friendliness that reassured patients and encouraged the staff to confide in him, he was a useful source of information and he was certainly the main root of the busy hospital grapevine. Little happened at Hartlake that Jimmy did not know about. But he could not tell Ivor much about the red-haired junior on Currie Ward. She did not get herself talked about, apparently.

Then he had run into Joanne. They had known each other since her first days at Hartlake and at one time they had enjoyed a mild flirtation. They were still on friendly terms. He took the opportunity to ask her about Daisy's party and learned that it had been a riot. He had been on duty but he did not mean to miss the wedding when his friend and colleague, Gavin Fletcher, married the pretty second-year nurse from Fleming Ward.

Jo had lightly mourned the loss of her flatmate. Jesting, Ivor had offered to move in with her. Wrinkling her nose at him in light-hearted reproach, she had told him that she had already found another flatmate and asked him if he knew Patti Parkin . . .

Patti. Absurd little name. Youthful, feminine, rather appealing. He was terribly aware of her as they sat close in the crowded pub. The scent of her hair and those striking green eyes and the nearness of her played havoc with his susceptible senses. She was a very exciting woman. He wondered if she knew it.

He smiled at her, replacing his glass. 'That pretty face wasn't made for scowling,' he teased.

'Nor for smiling at strangers,' she returned promptly, refusing to be coaxed into friendliness.

'I'm not a stranger, girl. You just don't recognise me without my white coat. Doctors are faceless creatures, you see. But we turn into human beings off the ward.'

'On or off the ward, you're a registrar and I'm a first year and never the twain shall meet,' Patti said firmly, needing a reason for her unreasonable resistance to his obvious interest. 'I don't mean to be hauled before Matron for flouting the rules.'

'She's human, too—and a woman,' he drawled. 'She'd understand that you were tempted beyond endurance by my charms.'

Patti looked quickly, discovered warm mischief dancing in the dark eyes. She smiled reluctantly. But she liked a man who could mock his own reputation. 'I don't think you *could* tempt me,' she told him, believing it. 'Sorry.'

'Couldn't I . . . ?' His smile deepened. His voice softened with a melting persuasion. He laid his hand over the slender fingers that rested on the table, toying with her glass. 'Try me . . .'

She thought he was joking. It was an absurd conversation, after all. Then their eyes met and something very like an electric shock rippled along her spine at the glow of desire in those dark depths, the stirring touch of his hand. She looked away, startled, alarmed by that wild flutter of her heart and the unexpected triggering of her senses in response to his look, his touch. 'No, thanks,' she said firmly, withdrawing her hand. She turned to speak to Jo.

But, determined to dismiss Ivor Maynard as a rake with only one thing in mind where any girl was concerned, she was much too aware of him. He was very attractive and very male, she thought ruefully. She might not like him or his type, but it was not as easy as she supposed to overlook his magnetism.

For one thing, he was much too handsome. For another, he was much too sure of himself.

The dark hair waved across his brow and sprang crisply from the temples and curled tightly at the nape of his neck. He wore it a little too long, she thought critically, as he leaned forward in response to a remark from John. She found herself wondering how many women had twined their fingers in those teasing black curls and resisted a foolish impulse to do the same thing.

It was a warm evening. He was casually dressed in jeans and an open-necked shirt, looking younger and even more attractive than when he toured the wards in his white coat. A heavy gold chain was bright against the strong column of his throat. There was the hint of dark, curling hair beneath the shirt. He was very much a man—and a renewed and unwelcome awareness of his masculinity, his stirring sensuality, rippled through her again.

Patti was astonished. Dark men had never appealed to her. Every man had always compared unfavourably with Steve in the past, she thought with a sudden pang. Fair good looks and bright blue eyes and the stocky athletic build of the rugger player had always been her blueprint for masculine sex appeal. Ivor Maynard had dark hair and dark eyes. He was lean and lithe and stamped with the kind of arrogance that she most despised in a man. He was so obviously a successful rake who preferred indoor sports, she thought dryly. So why did she feel that tug of physical attraction where he was concerned? She did not even like him!

Perhaps she was just lonely, missing Steve more

than usual. Sometimes, particularly in the company of couples, it was real anguish to recall the futile years of loving, the hopes and dreams that had turned to dust. Sometimes, she ached desperately to turn back the clock, to know again the comfort and content of Steve's arms about her, Steve's need of her. Now, tired after the day on the ward, she was at her most vulnerable. She found herself foolishly tempted by another man's interest and admiration and that stirring sexual desire. But she did not want to get involved with any man except in the way of friendship, she reminded herself firmly. Once bitten, twice shy . . .

Ivor did not seem bothered by her rebuff. She doubted if anything bothered the light-hearted and easy-going registrar very much. He was friendly, pleasant, chatting lightly to her in between taking part in the general conversation. They might have known each other for ever, she thought, and wondered if they seemed like a couple to any interested observer. His manner implied that they had slipped easily into friendship and Patti discovered that she did not object to that. She knew how to cope with amorous advances if they arose, after all. She was not an innocent schoolgirl. It did not appear very likely at the moment, she decided, and felt a vague and very foolish disappointment.

He looked tired, too, she thought, studying him. There was a hint of strain in that handsome face and a tell-tale nerve throbbed in the lean jaw. Many more demands were made on a surgeon than on a student nurse, of course. Lives really depended on his skill and sensitivity, his trained instinct for knowing when things were going wrong and his ability to put them right. Who could blame him if he was inclined to live it up as a release from the tensions of his work as a busy registrar?

He was said to be a clever and caring surgeon. Patti looked at his hand on the table, almost touching her own. Broad, long-fingered, muscular. A man's hand, strong and capable . . . a surgeon's hand. She visualised it wielding the healing knife. She remembered its firm grip on her arm the previous day, almost bruising. She recalled his touch of her hand, warm and meaningful and with a hint of tenderness.

She had discovered why he had a reputation for being a dangerous rake. He had a very potent effect on the senses. His kiss, his touch, might easily go to a girl's head like too much wine, Patti thought wryly. Knowing that he had suddenly become a threat, even to her level head, she was even more determined to keep him at a safe distance.

'Jo tells me that you'll be sharing her flat when Daisy gets married,' he said suddenly, turning to her. 'We shall be neighbours. I've a flat in Clifton Street, too . . . just a few doors down.'

'Very convenient.' For his work, she intended to imply. The narrow side street ran in conjunction to the hospital.

'Yes, I think so.' His smile was warm, slightly teasing. He knew perfectly well what her words had meant. 'We'll be able to see each other on and off the ward.'

'That isn't what I mean,' she said hastily. 'I won't have much time for socialising.'

'Hard-working nurses need to relax and recuperate in their free time. I can prescribe a very good tonic,' he told her, eyes twinkling.

A little colour sprang into her cheeks. There was no need to pretend that she did not know what he suggested. 'From all I hear about your brand of medicine it leaves a nasty taste in the mouth,' she returned, slightly tart. It was unlike her to slap anyone down so hard, but she was unsure of herself, alarmed because he evoked emotions that had lain dormant and which threatened to overwhelm her.

'You don't mean to let a few evil-minded gossips spoil what we have going for each other, surely,' he said softly. He touched her cheek with his long fingers. 'I want you, Patti . . .'

He was disconcertingly direct. She caught her breath. 'Well, I don't want you,' she said firmly, trying desperately to mean it.

'We shall see,' he murmured, eyes dancing.

He meant the light-hearted words as a kind of promise. To Patti, they seemed like a threat. His charm was insidious and his smile seemed to undermine all her resolution. It might be much too easy to warm to Ivor Maynard, to succumb to that undeniable charisma—and so it would be wise to keep him out of her life altogether, she felt. She doubted if it was anything more than just a game to him, anyway, a meaningless attempt at the flirtation for which he was famous. He was probably not really interested in her. By all accounts, he liked them very young and too innocent to know that they trod a dangerous path when they became involved with the Hartlake Heartbreaker!

Another couple came into the pub for a last drink before closing time and joined them. The girl slipped into John's seat as he went to the bar and smiled at Ivor.

'Where were you on Wednesday?' she challenged. 'You missed a great party.'

'So I hear. I was duty registrar.'

'Then I shall have to forgive you, I suppose. But it wasn't the same without you.' Her eyes were warm with affection, invitation. 'A little bird told me that you were with Jenefer Neal. That didn't please me at all!' She was teasing, doubting that there was foundation for the gossip about him and the staff nurse. It was probably just another of the absurd rumours that people were so ready to believe about him. She had known Ivor a long time and she was fond of him and she knew that he was far from being as black as he was painted. But it amused him to have the world think so, she knew.

He smiled, wryly. 'It would have been a more enjoyable evening, certainly. I spent most of it patching up a young motor-cyclist. Hopefully, he'll do. He's still in the IC Unit. His girl friend wasn't so lucky.' He sighed. 'Why do these kids take such risks? He's barely eighteen. She was fifteen.' He shook his head. 'Tragic . . .'

He really cared, Patti thought, warming to him. Pain touched the dark eyes and echoed in the deep, lilting voice. He was dedicated to saving life, of course. It must hurt him to see it thrown away by careless or stupid behaviour. It hurt Patti, too. Death was only acceptable for the very old or the incurably ill.

Felicity smiled at her. 'You were at the party. I remember that hair.'

Patti smiled back. 'People do!'

Felicity laughed. 'You're a nurse, aren't you? Which ward? I'm in Out-Patients.'

'Currie.'

'Oh, then you know Jenefer Neal,' she said quickly. 'How do you get on with her?'

'Not at all.' Patti was honest, wry.

'Really? She's a disciplinarian, I'm told. Another Sister Booth in the making. Does she tell you that you're too lax with the juniors? It seems to be her theme song!'

'I am a junior,' Patti said. 'First year . . .'

She was used to the surprise that leaped to the girl's eyes. Her obvious maturity often led people to suppose that she was state registered if they saw her out of uniform. She was used to being dismissed by slightly superior senior nurses, too, she thought dryly, as Felicity Hall turned back to Ivor.

They obviously knew each other well and their affection and understanding were very evident. Patti wondered if the staff nurse was another flame from his past. According to rumour, he had worked his way through each new set of juniors for years! Patti did not believe he had been that busy and still managed to reach the responsible position of registrar. No doubt his affairs had been very much exaggerated. But he was certainly attractive to women and one only had to observe and recognise that stirring sensuality to know that he would take advantage of any opportunity that offered.

Now. Felicity Hall was leaning towards him,

warm and inviting and responsive, and he was reacting to her like any red-blooded male, Patti noticed. John and Joanne had their heads together like lovers. The other couple in the party were engaged. She suddenly felt very much alone and desperately lonely. She was tired and missing Steve and she had to admit that there was an aching void in her life without him. Everyone she knew had someone special, someone who cared. She had no one.

After all, it seemed that nursing was not enough. She was young, and a woman, and she missed the warm reassurance of a man's affection and concern and company. Friendship was not enough.

She still loved Steve. But her life no longer revolved about him and all her dreams were dust. Why should she feel guilty because another man had the unexpected power to stir her senses? Why should she hold every man at arms' length because of a misguided and futile sense of loyalty? It was good to feel wanted again when she had given so gladly to Steve only to have it thrown back at her without warning. She sighed . . .

Ivor's keen ears caught that soft sound. He turned, caught just a glimpse of bleak misery in the green eyes, hastily veiled. Scarcely knowing her, he felt that he wanted to put an arm about her and chase away the shadows with a word, a smile, perhaps a comforting kiss. He felt an oddly protective concern towards her, a touch of tenderness—and that surprised him. For making love to a pretty girl was much more in his line than offering comfort, he reminded himself dryly.

He suspected that a man was to blame for that sigh, that look, that hedgehog prickliness in response to his interest. Joanne was her friend, but she had not seemed to be able to tell him much about Patti except that she discouraged every man from becoming anything more than a friend or useful escort for social occasions. A girl as pretty and as feminine and as desirable as Patti could have only one reason for keeping men at arms' length, he knew.

She was intent on keeping him at arms' length, too, he thought ruefully. Well, she was just another girl. Nothing special. A girl who did not want to know. Life was too short to waste any of it in chasing a girl who still sighed for another man. There was always Jenefer and Felicity and Marian and half a dozen other women only too willing to fall into his arms. Patti would just have to be the one that got away . . .

Can't win 'em all, he told himself with his usual, light-hearted philosophy—and wondered why he felt that he had particularly wanted to win this one. Meeting his eyes as he glanced at her, Patti smiled —the swift, spontaneous smile that had enchanted him before. It was unexpected, very effective. From being nothing special, she suddenly assumed an importance that took him unawares.

For his heart had turned over.

Ivor knew it was a medical impossibility. He knew it was the silly kind of thing that girls liked to read about in books, magazines. Hearts did nothing of the kind, of course. Yet it had happened. There was no other way to describe that odd, meaningful sensation. His heart had quite definitely somersaulted.

He was shaken to the core of his being. He had known that he liked the first-year nurse with her copper curls. He had been aware that she attracted him strongly with her pretty face and slender figure with its neat waist and tilting breasts. He had felt drawn to her maturity, her confidence, her level-headed refusal to be swayed too easily by his attentions. He had not realised that it would be dangerously easy to fall in love with her!

Ivor was thirty and he had never before felt that he could commit himself so totally and so irrevocably to any woman. He had done his best to resist the emotion that might threaten his whole way of life, his freedom, his contentment with the way things were and his ambitions for the future. He had always been reluctant to revise all that he had ever thought and felt about the necessity of any one woman to his happiness and satisfaction.

But that glowing smile hinted at a warmth and a sweetness and an enchantment that might ensnare a man almost against his will . . .

CHAPTER FOUR

TAKEN aback, Ivor quite forgot to smile with his usual responsive readiness and he was glad to turn away when Felicity spoke to him. It gave him the chance to come to terms with that new and not immediately acceptable emotion.

Patti's smile had been instinctive, to hide the heartache that might be lurking in her eyes. She had done her best to forget it in hard work. She had made new friends in new surroundings. She had found that hearts might ache but did not really break. Now, suddenly, she had learned that it was still possible to welcome the warmth and reassurance of another man's affection and desire.

She did not realise the impact of that smile on Ivor's heart. She only saw his dismissal of it, the ready way he turned to the other girl—and she wondered with a little pang of dismay if she had rebuffed him too successfully.

Jim Carver called "time" and there was a flurry of movement as drinks were downed and goodnights exchanged.

Joanne suggested going back to her flat for coffee. The night was still young, she declared. Patti's resolve to have just one drink and return to her books seemed to have melted away, but she was determined to part with her friends at this point. There was no incentive to remain for Ivor Maynard had abruptly lost interest. She did not mind, she told herself firmly. If she was recovering from Steve sufficiently to take an interest in other men, there were plenty of them who were more reliable and less dangerous at Hartlake. Why should she want to tangle with someone like Ivor Maynard?

They crossed the always-busy High Street in a group and Patti unexpectedly found Ivor by her side, taking her arm to guide her safely through the stream of traffic. 'I hope you don't mean to run away,' he said lightly. 'It isn't so late, Patti.'

It was a soft sound, her name on his lips, almost an endearment. She was surprised, oddly pleased, but puzzled by the man who seemed to blow hot and cold by turn. When they reached the other pavement, he transferred his clasp to her hand so naturally that it was a moment before she realised. But she did not pull away.

There was a comfort in the strong fingers curving about her own that she sorely needed, and she could not help a little glow of feminine satisfaction at the attention. She did not mean to be flattered, but she could not help being pleased. Perhaps it was weak and foolish, but what did she gain by holding out against a very attractive man who liked her? She was lonely and he offered a little balm for an aching heart, however briefly.

She helped Jo to make the coffees, hand them round. The small flat was one of several in the tall, terraced house that was only a stone's throw from the hospital. They were all occupied by nurses. Jo often declared that it was little more than an extension of the Nurses' Home with none of its irksome restrictions. There was always someone to make a cup of tea or enjoy a gossip or talk shop or even lend a pound in an emergency. Patti was looking forward to moving in with her lively, popular friend.

The dark-haired Felicity had settled herself comfortably and as close as she could get to Ivor on the rather shabby sofa. She was making him laugh with an anecdote about a patient when Patti handed his coffee. He smiled at her briefly. There was nothing special in the way he glanced, smiled. He was much too involved with the other girl.

She returned to the kitchen for her own coffee, stifling a stir of resentment. He flirted with any girl at the drop of a hat, of course. The women threw themselves at him and he responded as any man would who had no loyalty to any particular woman.

She was glad that he could not know how disturbing she found him. It was only a superficial attraction that could be soon forgotten, fortunately. It was ridiculous to suppose that she was vaguely hurt by his fickle behaviour or jealous of his attentions to someone else.

Patti turned as he came into the tiny kitchen. He seemed very tall, very close in that limited space—and she suddenly realised that her heart was beating too fast, quickened by the glow of intent in those dark eyes.

He smiled at her and took the coffee cup out of her hand. He set it down on the draining board by the sink. 'I can't kiss you with your hands full, girl.'

Patti's chin went up before that cool confidence. 'You can't kiss me at all!' she retorted promptly and turned towards the door.

He blocked the way. 'I can have a damn good try . . .' He put his arms about her and drew her close.

Patti knew it would be undignified to struggle—and she knew from experience that any resistance would only serve as a challenge. It would be more to the point to prove that she was utterly indifferent to that persuasive warmth in his dark eyes.

His mouth was warm and gentle, seeking the response that she refused to give. He kissed her. She would not kiss him.

Ivor lifted his head, looked into the sparkling, militant eyes. 'That isn't the way it should be, girl,' he said softly, reproachful, and for the first time Patti caught the faint trace of Welsh accent in his deep voice.

She hardened her heart. 'That's the way it is.' But cold though her lips and eyes and tone might be, her body betrayed her, tingling with that swift excitement. It was foolish. It was dangerous. But she was tempted to melt against him, to invite the kisses and caresses that might unleash a tidal flow of passion. She missed the warmth of loving that Steve had wrapped about her for so long. She did not expect to find it again with Ivor Maynard, or any other man. But was it so wrong to want to feel like a woman once more?

Her heart ached for Steve. Her body longed for him. There was the promise of ease in this man's arms that might bridge the gulf between despair and acceptance. Tempted, she resisted with all her might.

Disappointed, Ivor let her go. It did not seem to

him that she was as indifferent as she pretended. At the same time, he did not think she was merely playing hard to get. Instinctively he recognised a need that she sought to stifle. Was she just reluctant to become involved with someone who had a reputation for light loving? She did not know him. She had no reason to trust him, he reminded himself dryly.

Patti was disappointed, too. Taking her coffee, she escaped and went to talk to Joanne. Ivor Maynard returned to his seat by Felicity and the girl slipped her hand into his arm, smiling. His response was immediate, very warm—and typical of a man who took whatever came his way, Patti thought dryly, telling herself that she had no reason or right to dislike the probability that they would end the night in each other's arms. His way of life, his morals, was of no interest to her, after all . . .

Later, she said goodnight to Joanne and slipped out of the flat. She doubted if anyone had noticed that she had gone.

She was mistaken.

She had not gone a dozen yards along the quiet and rather dingy street in the shadow of the hospital when she heard footsteps, quick and determined. She turned.

'Walking these streets on your own at night isn't clever,' Ivor told her, annoyed. 'Why didn't you say that you wanted to go home?'

She raised an eyebrow. 'Because it didn't occur to me that it was anyone's concern but mine. No one is responsible for me, you know.'

'There are some unsavoury characters about at this hour.'

'And I shall be quite safe with you, I suppose?' She mocked his recent attempt to kiss her in the tiny kitchen.

Ivor smiled suddenly, a devil dancing in his dark eyes. 'As safe as you want to be . . .'

Something in his smile, his lazy drawl, caused Patti to quicken. Did he know that she found him much too attractive for peace of mind, she wondered wryly. No doubt he did. That kind of sensitivity must be built in to the nature of a rake —and made him all the more dangerous.

As they walked on, he took her hand as though he had every right to do so . . . and Patti discovered that she was warmed and reassured by that firm clasp. She knew she should withdraw her hand, insist that she did not need his escort, snub him so severely that he would really accept that she meant her claim of indifference. But she was quite unable to resist the tug of his physical magnetism.

She had met plenty of men since coming to Hartlake and some of them had become her good friends. Not one of them had ever stirred her senses as this man did. She knew it was foolish, dangerous. But she was not a green girl and there was no fear that she would lose her head over a man with far too much charm . . .

Patti overslept the next morning.

Late for Report, she hurried to join the nurses grouped about the desk, murmuring a hasty apology. She drew up a chair and produced pen and notebook from her apron pocket. It would be

Sister's morning off, she thought ruefully, aware of Jenefer Neal's icy disapproval.

The staff nurse waited until she was settled, very pointedly. Then she said coldly: 'I'll speak to you after Report, Nurse Parkin.' Her tone was ominous.

Much of Report did not concern someone as junior as Patti, but she listened carefully and made notes and wished she had not spent much of the night thinking about Ivor Maynard.

The feelings he evoked had nothing to do with loving, she knew—and in view of his reputation, it was just as well! She was made of sterner stuff than the vulnerable juniors who had apparently lost more than their hearts to the very attractive doctor in the past.

For one thing, she had no heart to lose. Or her virginity, she reminded herself. Loving Steve, sure that they would marry one day, she had given gladly, generously, eager to please and delight him. Her only regret was that all her loving, all her giving, all her patient loyalty, had counted for nothing when he met and married her cousin Valerie within a few weeks. Patti had done her best to understand, to accept. But it had hurt—and it went on hurting.

Nursing fulfilled a need to be busy, to be needed, to have a purpose in life. She was often too tired to dwell on the might-have-been when she slipped between the sheets at the end of a long day. But nothing really eased the ache of loneliness or, worst of all, the terrible feeling that she had been found wanting in some way. She had given with all her heart, but Steve had never really loved her and he had dismissed the sexual relationship between them as though it had never been very important. He had managed to make her feel cheap. Patti would always love him, but she did not think she could forgive him for that.

She had come to Hartlake with the resolution not to let disappointment spoil everything for her. At the same time, she did not think of replacing Steve with any other man. She could only love once in a lifetime, she felt.

Without conceit, Patti knew that she was pretty and that men admired her. She had grown fond of one or two men that she had met at Hartlake. But they were only friends and she did not feel that they could ever be anything more.

Patti had always believed that the thrill of desire and the urgent need for its fulfilment was not possible for her unless she loved. So it came as a shock to realise the impact of Ivor Maynard on her senses. She knew it was only the sudden spark of infatuation, a wanton sexuality that excited and shocked at the same time. She did not really like him. She did not really know him. Yet she hungered for his kiss and the strength of his arms and she was weak with wanting when she thought of the power and the glory she might find in his embrace.

Was it any wonder that she had scarcely slept for that persistent ache of longing for a near-stranger?

'You can do the pulse and temps round, Nurse Parkin—and don't take all day over it. There's no time for gossiping this morning. We're short of a junior as well as Sister and there's a lot to be done!'

Patti wrenched her mind back to the present at the sound of Jenefer Neal's sharp voice. 'Yes, Staff . . .'

The staff nurse swept the pile of folders from the desk into her arms. One fell to the floor, scattering its contents. Trying to be helpful, Patti scrambled for them. Jenefer Neal took the restored folder from her without a word of thanks.

'Straighten your cap—and I doubt very much if that was a clean apron this morning. See that you change it before you begin the round.' She sighed heavily. 'I honestly don't know why you came into nursing when you've neither the inclination nor aptitude for the ordinary basics like punctuality and cleanliness. You may have come to this ward from Fleming with a good report, but I can only assume that they don't maintain *our* standards!'

As she stalked off, Patti smiled wryly in response to a warmly sympathetic glance from Marian Foster.

'I wouldn't be in your shoes for anything,' the third-year said with feeling.

Patti shrugged. 'It's only nit-picking. She can't find any real fault with my work.'

'She will,' Marian prophesied in doom-laden tones. 'She's furious with you. Weren't you out with the dishy Ivor Maynard last night? She fancies him and he's been stringing her along for weeks!'

Patti was dismayed that facts could be so distorted by the gossips. 'Don't tell me that's all over the hospital!' She hoped that Ivor would not suppose that she had been boasting of his interest.

'Well, of course! No such thing as a private life in

this place,' Marian declared, a little surprised to have confirmation of the gossip. She had thought that Patti had too much sense to tangle with the good-looking but very rakish registrar. 'I expect everyone knows the details of your entire evening by this time!'

'Then everyone must have found it a very boring recital,' Patti retorted dryly. 'Nothing happened.'

Marian raised an eyebrow. 'Look, love, we're talking about Ivor Maynard,' she said, amused. 'It isn't possible that nothing happened.'

'We're talking about me,' Patti said firmly. 'It isn't only possible but definite!'

She wished that he wasn't such a womaniser. A girl had only to be seen in his company and it was assumed that he had made another conquest. He was a charmer with a disarming smile and a very persuasive manner and it was easy to believe that he was seldom thwarted in his amorous pursuit of a girl. Yet he had left her the previous night without a kiss or even the tentative suggestion that they should meet again. Patti did not know what to make of his casual, almost cavalier attitude.

She went to do the round, bright and cheerful and interested despite her inner turmoil. Heeding Jenefer Neal's words, she went quickly from bed to bed, but still managed a few friendly words with most patients. Every one was an individual who felt that his case was "special" if not unique. All patients firmly believed that each nurse and doctor, however junior, had the details of his or her case at their finger-tips. A good nurse needed an excellent memory as well as caring concern and genuine compassion. Even so, it was routine to check the patient's chart that hung on the bottom rail of each bed when first coming on duty each day.

Nurses were often accused of being hard and insensitive. Such people did not come into nursing or left within a few weeks. A nurse simply had to acquire an extra skin if she was to survive the work. Pain and distress and often death were hard lessons in life for a young girl to learn and student nurses were seldom prepared for the many demands of the work. But pain could be alleviated and the distressed could be comforted and even death was not so terrible if it was looked squarely in the face. Life and death walked side by side on the wards and in the hospital corridors and became equally familiar faces to the staff during the course of their work.

A nurse also learned to adopt an air of cheerful optimism which never allowed a patient to know when he was really poorly. He was always "doing nicely" or would "soon be going home". The positive approach was very important. Patti had been born looking on the bright side, her family often declared—and it was a valuable asset. Her very presence on the ward seemed to bring a lift to the lowest spirits. It might not endear her to embittered staff nurses, but she was a favourite with the patients and many of the senior staff commented with approval on her qualities and her promise.

Patti never doubted that she would eventually wear the badge of a state-registered nurse. She was working hard to that end and she hoped very much that she would be offered a job as a staff nurse when she finished her training.

She loved Hartlake and she loved the involvement, the daily dramas and demands, the many rewards of nursing in a busy teaching hospital that catered for a vast area of London as well as patients sent from many parts of the country for specialist treatment. Finals were a long way off, of course. She had a great deal to learn and she was a very junior nurse . . .

Junior nurses scurried hither and thither at the bidding of the caustic Jenefer Neal and never thought of rebelling, Patti told herself firmly, trying to remember the next chore on her long list. She was doing the work of two juniors that morning. It felt like four!

She hurried to the linen cupboard. Two new admissions, Mr Balfour's incontinence and her own carelessness with a bowl of washing water meant four bed changes and no one to help her with them.

She came out of the roomy cupboard with her arms full of linen packs as Ivor turned the corner and came along the corridor towards her, white coat flying with the briskness of his stride.

Seeing him, her heart gave an absurd leap of delight. One of the plastic packs shifted, slid slowly to the floor. Balancing the others, Patti stooped to pick it up, glad to hide her suddenly flushed face. At almost the same moment, Ivor reached her and bent down. His broad shoulder brushed her bright head and knocked the precarious cap askew.

'Sorry . . .' He smiled at her.

'I can do without *you* this morning,' she declared, almost meaning it. She struggled with the slippery packs while trying to straighten her cap at the same time. Another fell to the floor. Laughter danced in his dark eyes as he retrieved it and Patti smiled, reluctantly. She could be cross with herself for the way her heart bumped in her breast, but it was difficult to be cross with him, she discovered. His charm was disarming and very dangerous.

'It just isn't my day,' she sighed.

'You look rushed.'

'I *am* rushed.'

He held open the swing doors of the ward for her to enter. 'Then this isn't the moment to ask you to have dinner with me?'

Patti glanced at him, quick, doubtful. She was tempted to accept an innocent-sounding invitation but she suspected that dinner might lead to a more dangerous pastime. She did not trust him any more than she trusted the kindling excitement that he evoked too easily.

'No,' she said, firmly.

His eyes danced. 'No, it isn't the moment? Or no, you won't take pity on a lonely and overworked doctor?'

She had no time to answer. Jenefer Neal bore down on them with a furious frown and Patti fled with her armful of linen packs.

Jenefer was cold, very formal. 'Good morning, Mr Maynard. Have you come to look at Mr Fielding? We're rather concerned about him this morning. Pulse and respiration are weak and he's retaining urine . . .'

Ivor nodded. 'Yes, let's have a look at him . . .' Instantly, he was all surgeon, the persistent liking and desire for a pretty redhead thrust to the back of his mind as he followed the staff nurse to the side ward and his patient.

Patti made beds and took round the morning drinks and admitted new patients and helped with dressings and Ivor was gone from the ward when she had time to think about him again.

Then she wondered if he had really meant that casual invitation. She wondered if she had really meant to turn it down. A decision had not been demanded of her and she was relieved. For she really did not know what to do about Ivor Maynard. She did not like the way her body responded to him without rhyme or reason. She felt it would be much too easy to become involved with him in an entirely physical relationship. It was no part of her code for living, she reminded herself firmly.

But she recalled the warm clasp of his hand and the hint of tenderness in the touch of his lips on her own, and the smile in those dark eyes which seemed to promise something more than just a brief and promiscuous interlude.

It was very tempting to wonder if she could find a little balm for the heartache of losing Steve in the obvious interest of another man . . . even if that man did have a reputation for light and meaningless loving. She would not be risking her heart or her happiness. And she would not need to worry about Ivor's heart. She doubted if his kind knew what it meant to love anyone for real . . .

CHAPTER FIVE

AN afternoon lecture released Patti from the ward for a few hours and she was glad to escape from Jenefer Neal's dislike and disapproval. She was not going to be easily forgiven for being seen with Ivor Maynard on the previous evening, she thought ruefully. Nor for the warmth in his smile that morning, unmistakably noticed and resented by the staff nurse.

After the lecture, she took advantage of a break to relax in the hospital garden with the other girls in her set. It was a glorious afternoon, warm and sunny without a cloud in the very blue sky.

The square garden was surrounded by tall buildings and dominated by a central statue of Sir Henry Hartlake, the founder. A sheltered spot, it was a popular meeting place among the staff and much used as a short cut from one part of the hospital to another.

The group of first years in the distinctive check uniforms attracted a great deal of attention as they sat on the grass, talking and laughing and enjoying the summer sunshine and the moments of relaxation. Hartlake could compete with any other hospital for the prettiness and appeal of its nurses, Ivor thought as he strolled through the garden on his way to a conference.

He was not even thinking about Patti as he

glanced at the cluster of girls on the lawn. But the bright sun made a halo of her auburn curls and he noticed that she was not wearing her cap, unlike the others. It lay on the grass as though she had thrown it down impatiently. He smiled, well able to believe that the tiny cap was a constant trial to Patti and her seniors. Her curls were so thick and lively, gleaming in the sun.

She was smiling, animated and very pretty. Ivor admired the sparkle in the lovely eyes and caught the hint of infectious laughter in her voice as she called to one of her companions. Then she saw him and he thought a little colour came up in her face. Their eyes met and he smiled, paused at the edge of the path.

Patti hesitated. Then she scrambled to her feet and picked up her cap. 'I'd better go, girls,' she said lightly. 'I can't afford to be late back when Neal is on the warpath.' She walked across the lawn to where Ivor stood, so obviously waiting for her that she was a little disconcerted, knowing that it would lead to more talk. Reaching him, she smiled and said on a sudden impulse: 'No, it isn't the moment.' Just as though several hours had not intervened between question and answer.

Ivor laughed. He looked down at her with warm appreciation in his dark eyes. 'Then we have a date,' he said lightly. 'I'll call for you at eight o'clock.'

'Tonight!' It was unexpected, too soon. Patti didn't feel ready to commit herself to any kind of involvement, after all. She wondered what had prompted that impulsive remark. 'I shall fall asleep in the middle of the meal,' she protested.

'Then the handsome prince will wake the sleeping beauty with a kiss,' he told her, eyes twinkling.

'And probably turn into a frog,' she said, matter of fact. 'No, I can't make it this evening. Sorry...'

'Eight o'clock, Patti,' he said, very firm. 'I've already organised the meal.'

She watched him walk away, not knowing whether to be impressed or irritated by his cool confidence. He was obviously a man who made his plans in advance and did not like to be thwarted, she thought wryly. She wished she did not feel so drawn to him when she knew perfectly well that he was a rake with only one thing in mind. There was unmistakable intent in the way that his dark eyes rested on her face and figure. He wanted to get her into bed and no doubt he had already organised that part of the evening too, she thought. He would be sadly disappointed...

It was a long time since Patti had felt butterflies in the stomach when getting ready for a date. It was ridiculous, she knew—she did not even like Ivor Maynard very much. She wondered how it had come about that she was going out with him when she had resolved to keep him firmly at a distance.

And what to wear? She did not know where he was taking her, she realised. Patti went through the contents of her wardrobe and decided on a black pleated silk skirt and a filmy black blouse with a scooped neckline and very full sleeves.

Dressed, she surveyed herself in the mirror. Black enhanced the rich colouring of her hair and the creaminess of her skin and the glow of her green eyes.

She wrinkled her shapely nose at her reflection. 'You look very sexy,' she told herself. 'You're just asking for trouble with a man like Ivor Maynard!' She shrugged away a tiny qualm. She was not a green girl. She was sure that she could handle the situation if it threatened to get out of hand.

She was ready and waiting when his car drew up outside the Nurses' Home. She hurried to get in, feeling a dozen pairs of eyes on her back. It was a distinctive car and Ivor was a very distinctive man. More gossip for the grapevine, she thought. But she did not mean to worry about Jenefer Neal's probable punishment for a junior who dared to encourage the man she wanted for herself.

Ivor leaned across to open the car door and she slid into the seat beside him, heart thudding for absolutely no reason but the excitement of going out with a very attractive man. His eyes held admiration. She wondered if she betrayed her immediate reaction to the charm of his smile and the impact of his very good looks.

As she smiled at him, he leaned to kiss her, very lightly. Startled, Patti drew back. She was shaken by the warm, fleeting touch of his lips. 'Don't do that!' she exclaimed instantly, sharp. 'People are watching...'

'So?' The car slid gently away from the kerb.

'So it will be all over Hartlake that another first year is daft enough to fall into your arms,' she said bitterly.

He smiled. 'But you haven't.' He added softly,

mischievously: 'Yet . . .'

Her chin tilted. 'And won't!'

He drove past the main entrance to the hospital with its wide stone steps, turned left into Clifton Street. A little way along, he pulled the car into the kerb.

'Where are we going?' Patti asked, wondering if it was a convenient place to park while they went to one of the many foreign restaurants in the High Street.

'One of the best eating places in town,' he told her, smiling. 'Ask anyone.'

She looked from him to the terrace of tall houses and back again, doubtful. 'Your flat?'

'You look like a bird about to take flight,' Ivor said, amused. He touched her cheek with his fingers. It was almost but not quite a caress. 'Come and have your dinner before you fly away. I'm a very good cook and I've gone to a lot of trouble to please you.'

'Without a thought of reward, of course!' she retorted, very dry.

The dark eyes danced. 'Now don't be naive, Patti. I'm setting you up for the big seduction scene, naturally,' he drawled.

She smiled, reluctantly. He had taken the wind out of her sails with the light words. 'I suspect that's true . . .'

She was surprised when he ushered her into the comfortable and welcoming flat. It was not at all what she had expected. It was tastefully and expensively furnished with thick carpets on the floors and heavy drapes at the windows. She approved his taste in the fine prints on the walls and the few good pieces of porcelain. It was a man's flat stamped with his personality and the evidence of wealth.

Ivor gave her a drink and switched on the stereo and went into the kitchen to check the progress of the meal.

Patti wandered about the sitting-room, looking at his books, his pictures, his records. Then she sat on the wide leather sofa, wishing she felt more at ease. He was very much a stranger, of course. She knew very little about him. She knew his reputation —that ought to be enough to put her off him completely, she thought wryly . . . and wondered why it did not. In fact, she found him much too attractive for comfort.

Restless, she followed him out to the neat and well-equipped kitchen. 'Anything I can do?'

'Not a thing.' His eyes were warm as he looked down at her. He was a tall man, over six foot. Even the high heels of her thin-strapped shoes did not bring her head above his broad shoulders. She was small and slight with an air of fragility that was probably deceptive. For nurses had to be tougher than they often looked. 'Everything's under control,' he added, smiling. Even the feelings that came close to overwhelming him where this girl was concerned, he thought, knowing that he must not rush his fences. He sensed she was not at all sure about him. But it was encouraging that she had accepted his invitation. For all his seeming confidence, Ivor had not really expected that she would. He was a little anxious that the evening should be a success. It was very important that she should like him, trust him. He could not shake off the feeling that Patti was meant to become something special in his life. He hoped he was going to get close enough to her to prove it!

'This is a new experience,' Patti said brightly. 'Whenever I'm invited to a man's place for a meal I usually find that I'm expected to cook it!'

'I won't even expect you to wash up,' he promised.

'Now that *is* spoiling me!'

Ivor laughed. Then he put his arms about her, very gently, drew her towards him. 'No one to see now, girl,' he said softly and kissed her. It was the merest breath of a kiss.

Patti clenched her hands against his hard chest, resisting him with her entire body. Her mouth quivered but would not warm to the touch of his lips. For she was filled with sudden, fierce wanting and she knew that she had very little defence against this man. She must not melt into the arms that were holding her so lightly, only hinting at the delights to be found in lovemaking. He was too experienced, too clever, she thought ruefully. He knew just how to stir a woman to swift, aching desire while seeming to make no demands on her at all.

Her resistance was a solid barrier between them. Ivor knew better than to force her to response. But he was determined to coax her into soft, sighing surrender in the very near future. He wanted her so much. He recognised the answering urgency in that slight body for all her obvious determination to pretend that it did not exist.

Ivor released her and turned to stir the sauce as though it was of much greater importance than her reluctance to be kissed.

'Don't distract the chef,' he said lightly. 'This sauce is my *piéce de resistance*!'

Patti liked him for making light of an awkward moment. The evening might have foundered at that point because of her refusal to enjoy his embrace. He did not seem to mind. No doubt he was used to reluctant young nurses who needed to be coaxed into bed, she thought dryly.

She did not think he could hurt her. It was necessary to love a man to be hurt when he walked out of one's life as Ivor inevitably would when his fancy turned to another pretty face. Patti doubted if he or any man could touch her heart sufficiently for it to matter. But he could drag her pride in the dust all over again. She could give as she had given before only to realise how little it meant to the man while it created a bond that a woman did not forget even if she lived to be an old, old lady.

It was ironic that Ivor had such a potent effect on her emotions that the mere touch of his hand caused a havoc of desire. She longed for his love-making and wondered if he could transport her to the ecstatic heights that she had always failed to reach in Steve's embrace.

Loving Steve, she had given gladly, but she had never been sexually stirred by him and that had been a constant anxiety and regret. Wanting to please and delight him, she had never enjoyed sex with him. She had told herself that she was inhibited by her very strict upbringing and that marriage would cure her seeming frigidity. But Steve had not married her, after all, and Patti was haunted by the conviction that her coldness was partly to blame.

Perhaps she would turn cold in Ivor's arms, too, if she was fool enough to fall into them. Perhaps she *was* frigid. It seemed to Patti that love and sexual longing should go hand in hand. Yet she loved Steve. She did not understand why her body should thrill to a man who meant nothing...

The meal proved his claim that he was a good cook. It was excellent. So was the wine that he served with it and Patti suspected that she drank more of it than she should. She said so, a little wryly.

Ivor twirled an imaginary moustache, eyes twinkling. 'All part of the plan, my dear,' he drawled. 'Ply her with wine and the girl will be mine...'

There was laughter in the dark eyes. The words were light, but Patti wondered if there was a grain of truth in them. Warmed by the wine, she was more relaxed, more at ease with him, although she was still anticipating the inevitable overtures. She hoped that she would have the strength of mind to resist them! She was beginning to like him, she knew. That was probably even more dangerous than the potency of his physical attractions.

'Not in this case,' she said firmly.

Ivor laughed, rose to his feet. 'Black coffee...?' he suggested.

She nodded. 'Please.' She followed him to the kitchen with the dirty plates. 'Why don't we wash up first, Ivor?'

'I'll do it later. I'm a dab hand with dishes,' he assured her, smiling. 'Sit down and relax and wait for your coffee.'

But Patti insisted on helping and found that the domestic chore created a kind of intimacy that was reassuring. He was too lavish with the liquid soap and seeing him with lather to his elbows and a dab of it on his cheek where he had brushed a strand of hair from his eyes quite dispelled the lurid image of him as a sex fiend who lured unsuspecting girls to his flat for an evening of debauchery.

Over coffee, they chatted to a background of music and discovered that they had several tastes and interests in common. They talked about Hartlake, too. He had a fund of amusing stories about past patients and Patti listened with interest, liking the sound of his deep voice and the way that laughter crinkled his dark eyes.

He was a registrar and she was a very junior nurse, but he did not make her feel that the gulf could not be bridged. Away from the hospital, they were just a man and a girl who wished to know more about each other. She was interested in his family, his background, his days as a medical student. She told him that she had been a secretary before deciding to nurse but she did not tell him just what had prompted her to leave home and loving family and well-paid job with a firm of estate agents. He did not probe and Patti was grateful. No one could have told him about her broken engagement because no one at Hartlake knew. She was not a whiner and she had not felt that anyone would be particularly interested in her heartache.

She was enjoying the evening with Ivor. She had not realised how much she missed the ordinary pleasure and intimacy of male company since she had been thrown so much among girls, many of them younger than herself. She had been used to spending much of her time with Steve, encouraging him to talk of his ambitious plans for the future, looking forward to sharing that future with him and never doubting that she would.

She missed Steve, so it was comforting to enjoy the company of a mature and charming and very personable man. And it was reassuring that Ivor seemed to enjoy her company, too. He might tease, but she felt that he did not really regard her as just another conquest. In fact, he seemed to be keeping his distance on that score, Patti thought, a little disappointed.

He was almost impersonal for all his warm friendliness. He did not behave in the least like a would-be seducer. He had not even tried to kiss her again. It was perverse to wish that he would when she had rebuffed him so plainly earlier in the evening, Patti told herself firmly. He probably felt that he was respecting her wishes. It was just as well that he did not suspect how much she longed to be in his arms.

Patti smiled at him, drowsy from food and wine and the warmth of the evening. She had kicked off her shoes and curled into a corner of the sofa, tucking her small, shapely feet beneath her.

Ivor's heart contracted. She looked like a sleepy child, pretty, vulnerable, very appealing. He was moved by the desire to draw her into his arms and hold her very close, without passion. He was taken aback by the feeling that for once did not seem to have its roots in sexual need.

He knew she would misinterpret his motives if he reached for her and he did not mean to rock the boat at this stage. They had laid the foundation for friendship and Ivor meant to be content with that for the time being.

'I think it's time I took you back to the Nunnery,' he said reluctantly, glancing at his watch. 'It's getting late . . .'

Patti agreed, but every instinct rebelled at such a tame end to the evening. She told herself firmly that she should be grateful that it had not been necessary to fight him off, after all. She reached for her shoes and thrust her feet into them. As she stood, the high heel of one shoe turned on the thick carpet, throwing her off balance. She clutched involuntarily at Ivor's arm, laughing at her own awkwardness. He steadied her, smiling . . . and as she looked up at him, Pattie found herself drowning in the warm depths of those dark eyes.

Something within her reached out to that promise of delight. Impulsively, she put her arm about his neck and drew his dark head down and brushed his lips with her own. He stiffened and she wondered if she had made a mistake. Perhaps he was not the kind of man to appreciate amorous overtures from a woman. He might prefer to make all the running, she thought.

But she kissed him again, trying to melt that surprising resistance. She sensed his mouth suddenly warm and quicken and then she was pulled almost roughly into his arms and kissed with an ardour that dispelled the fear that he did not want her as she wanted him.

They kissed with a mounting excitement and then Ivor drew her down to the sofa cushions, his body as urgent as her own with the passion that sought to sweep them beyond all boundaries. It was madness, Patti knew. But she was weak with wanting and there was too much magic in his kiss, the sigh of her name on his lips, the experienced touch of his hand as he explored and caressed the curves of her breast beneath the thin blouse.

She did not want to resist the slow, sensuous tide of wanting that threatened to engulf her. She clung to him with yielding in every line of her slender frame. She had never known so much eager longing, so much urgency of desire, so much certainty of the ecstatic fulfilment that her body craved and his body could provide . . .

Wanting her was a raging torrent of desire, a fierce fever in Ivor's blood. It would be the easiest thing in the world to take her, he knew. She was eager, entirely willing, more responsive than he had ever dreamed she might be. There had been no need to coax this girl into surrender. She had hurled herself into his arms with an amazing intensity of yearning.

Ivor wondered why he hesitated. What was wrong with him, for heaven's sake? Had he suddenly turned puritan? He was an ardent man and he had never scorned what the gods offered in the past. He had lost count of the girls who had lain and loved in his sensual arms.

Somehow, Patti was special. She was a different

kind of enchantment. He simply could not take her as lightly and as carelessly as he had taken all those other girls. Casual sex and Patti just did not seem to go together, he discovered. She was a whole new world of commitment. He was not yet ready for it, he felt.

Holding her, his kiss turned tender and the hand that cradled her soft breast became still. His embrace gradually lost its fire, its urgency. Patti sensed the dying of the flame and was incredulous, angry, bitterly disappointed. Her body throbbed with the excitement and the need that he had evoked and he was abruptly cold, lacking inclination. She had been more than eager for his loving and he had rejected her at the very moment when he might have taken her over the threshold into that glorious fulfilment!

CHAPTER SIX

DEEPLY humiliated, shamed by her own intensity of passion and his lack of it, Patti thrust him away and scrambled to her feet. With trembling hands, she thrust her blouse into the waistband of her skirt and brushed the tumbled curls from her flushed face.

'Well, you certainly lived up to your reputation!' she declared lightly as though he was entirely to blame for that passionate interlude and she had been reluctant in his arms. 'I was a fool to trust you!' She desperately needed to create the illusion that the wanting had been all on his side. She did not think she could bear him to know the blow he had struck at her pride, her confidence, her self-respect.

She had thrown herself at him only to be rejected. What did she lack that all the other women in his life had apparently possessed? She wondered with welling bitterness, the near-despair of frustration. Where did she fail? *He* could not accuse her of coldness, of lack of response!

Perhaps she had been too eager. Perhaps, like many men, he preferred the challenge of virginal reluctance and resistance, enjoying the chase almost more than the conquest. Perhaps he had simply been repelled by her wanton willingness to enjoy a sexual encounter with a man who was little more than a stranger.

Ivor saw that the lovely green eyes were suspiciously bright for all the airy words and her apparent composure. She was very near to tears. He knew that he had hurt and disappointed her. He was not an insensitive or stupid man. Too late, he had realised just how she would interpret that exercise of self-control!

He ran a hand through his dark hair, smiling in rueful apology. 'You're too much temptation, girl . . .' he drawled, as though he had urged and she had drawn back instead of the other way around. Deliberately, he aided and abetted the deception, sensing that she needed to believe it for reasons of her own.

Patti managed a smile. He was being kind, she thought bitterly—and that was even greater humiliation. Suddenly it seemed very necessary to show that she was indifferent to this man.

'Then I'll keep temptation out of your way in future,' she said lightly but implacably.

A frown leaped to his eyes. 'I hope that doesn't mean what I think it means.'

'It's been a nice evening. I've enjoyed it,' she said truthfully. 'But I don't want to repeat it, Ivor,' she added, hoping he would not recognise a blatant lie and call her bluff.

'Oh, Patti . . .' He reached for her.

She eluded him quickly. 'I mean it.' She would not look at him. She would not risk the slightest touch of his hand for fear she might betray her aching need of him. She scarcely knew him. She did not even know that she liked him more than a little. But she melted inside with sheer longing for his kiss, his embrace, that sensual but sensitive love-making with all its magical promise.

One glance at that small, set face told Ivor not to persist. This was not the moment or the mood, he thought ruefully.

'If that's the way you want it,' he said with a slight shrug of his broad shoulders. Women could be the very devil. But this woman was not simply playing hard to get. She was too obviously stirred—and just as obviously frightened of the passion that had leaped between them.

Patti had not expected him to protest. He might even be relieved. But it hurt that he could accept so readily, almost indifferently.

She was startled and rather dismayed by that little pang. She had never wanted or expected to be hurt again by any man. Did she like this one so much so soon? Just as well that she had made a stand here and now, perhaps . . .

They walked to the Nurses' Home in the High Street. Patti pointed out that it was not worth using his car for such a short distance. He said very little as they walked. She talked too much, emptily, defensively.

She paused a few yards from the tall building. 'Don't come any further, Ivor . . .'

He understood. She did not want to be seen with him, to be talked about. He was too well-known. His reputation could be a considerable drawback at times, he thought wryly.

'Very well.'

Patti held out her hand with an air of finality. 'Goodnight.'

Ivor was torn. He could let her walk out of his life as she seemed to wish—or he could admit that she was much too important to him and make some attempt to hold on to her. It was not an easy admission for a man who had always valued and enjoyed his freedom and was not too sure that he was ready to relinquish it for any woman.

He wished he knew how she really felt about him. He knew how her body responded to him. He did not know at all what was going on in her mind or heart. She seemed so confident but he sensed that she was more vulnerable than most. She seemed so cool but he had kindled a fire that could blaze so hotly that it had almost consumed them both. It was a dangerous flame. Perhaps Patti knew that too well and did not mean to be scorched by it again. Perhaps he would be wise to follow her lead . . .

He took her hand. 'See you around, Patti . . .' He carried her hand to his lips and pressed a kiss into the palm, closed her fingers over it tightly, smiling.

The light words, the easy smile, seemed to rob the small gesture of any significance. But Patti continued to feel the tingling touch of his lips on her flesh as he strode away, a tall, distinguished and very distinctive figure. She looked after him, feeling bereft.

She slept deeply and without dreaming that night. It was the first time in years that she had slipped into sleep without Steve on her mind—and it was the first time that she had woken to the thought of another man.

She lay for a few minutes, remembering the evening with Ivor Maynard, recalling the discovery that he was a much nicer person than she had believed or expected him to be. Her heart quickened just a little at the prospect of seeing him on the ward or about the hospital later in the day. Then she remembered how they had parted.

The finality of her tone and the way she had held out her hand in that dismissive manner and his acceptance of his marching orders made her wonder if he would have a word or a smile for her when they encountered each other again.

He was a very attractive man and he did not need to bother with a girl who declared that she did not want to bother with him. Patti ransacked her memory to recall just what it was that she had said or done. *Something* had quenched that fierce and urgent passion so abruptly. Now, in the cool light of day, she could be grateful. She might not have liked him or herself very much this morning if things had turned out differently. Now, she could marvel at that tumult of wanting, like nothing she had ever known before, and tell herself that the wine had been much more potent than his physical attractions . . .

She ran up the stone steps of the main entrance to Hartlake and pushed through one of the glass doors into Main Hall, trim and pretty in her uniform and a new dancing lightness in her step of which she was totally unaware. But it caught the attention of the big man who sat in his usual place behind the Reception Desk, his fingers on the pulse of the big, busy, teaching hospital.

'Good morning, Nurse!' Jimmy called with a knowing smile and a wink for the pretty junior. He had seen too many young nurses with that particular brightness of eye and lightness of step not to know that romance was in the air. The little redhead might not know it but he certainly did!

Patti sent him one of her bright, warm smiles as she hurried by and it seemed to more than one observer that a golden ray of sunlight had found its way into that spacious but windowless area of the hospital.

She had slept well and woken refreshed and she was looking forward to the hectic but so enjoyable day on the wards. She loved nursing. She liked all its demands. It was interesting, absorbing, rewarding. Her heart was lighter than it had been for months. Patti did not consciously connect the lift of her spirits with Ivor Maynard. She genuinely believed that her eagerness to begin the day's work on the ward sprang from a love of nursing rather than the hope of seeing him.

She made her way to the third floor and Currie Ward, donned a crisp white apron and went to report to Sister. The ward was a bustle of activity with five patients due to go to Theatres that day. Mr Willis was among them, a pathetic little man in the voluminous white gown and socks, very pale, very frightened.

Breaking all the rules, Patti sat on the side of his bed and took his trembling hand in her own. 'You mustn't worry, Mr Willis,' she said with her warm, reassuring smile. 'Everything is going to be all right. You won't know a thing about it and when you wake up I'll be right here to say hallo.'

He shook his head. 'I won't be coming back to this ward, Nurse.'

'Yes, you will . . . and we'll look after you, get you well again.' She patted his hand, comforting him. 'Look how well Mr Deacon is getting on already after losing *both* legs . . .' And she nodded towards the elderly man who was bowling a wheelchair down the middle of the ward on his way to the day room, exchanging cheerful greetings with other patients en route. 'He's going home in a few days, you know. So will you be before you know it.'

He would not be cheered. 'You mean well, Nurse. But I won't come through this lot,' he said wanly. 'I can't take it, that's a fact . . . not on me own, I can't. If I still had me missus—well, that would be different. She'd 'ave seen me through it.' There were tears in the rheumy eyes. One spilled, trickled slowly down the thin cheek. The old man did not brush it away.

'*We'll* see you through it, Mr Willis,' Patti said gently. But she was troubled. There was no fighting spirit in the little man and she had learned in a few short months that it was vital to a patient's recovery. Without the will to live, a patient could sink lower and lower without apparent reason when the prognosis should have been complete recovery.

'I'd like you to be down there with me, Nurse.' Patients always spoke of "going down", either not knowing or not accepting that Theatres were situated on the top floor of the hospital. In the same way, patients still clung to the belief that all operating staff wore white gowns and masks although it was some years since green had been adopted as a more restful colour for the surgeons who spent so many hours beneath the arc lights of the theatres.

'Of course I will,' she soothed, determined to manage it by hook or by crook.

As a junior nurse, it was usually one of her roles to accompany a patient to Theatres and return for him when he was ready to leave the recovery room. Drowsy from the pre-med and then sent off to sleep by an injection in the ante-room, he would not know that she went back to the ward before the operation even began and most patients liked to feel that a familiar face went with them into Theatres. That kind of reassurance was a very important part of nursing, Patti had found. Every patient was apprehensive, a little lost without the support of family and friends, dependent as a child on the nurses and just a little distrustful of the doctors who held his life in their hands.

Jenefer Neal approached the bed, the look in her eye boding ill for the junior who flouted convention so blatantly. It was only just about permissible for a senior consultant to perch on the edge of a patient's bed if he was so minded. Sister might allow herself a tolerant smile at such times if he was a favourite but she would maintain an air of rigid disapproval if he was not. Visitors were either swiftly warned against the practice by those patients who knew the unwritten hospital rule or else cautioned by a passing nurse. Nurses never sat down in the presence of a patient except to special the very sick who were nursed in small side wards out of sight of other patients.

'Time for your pre-med, Mr Willis,' the staff nurse announced brightly. Her eyes narrowed as they rested on Patti who had hastily risen to her feet but still held tightly to the old man's hand. 'I thought I told you to turn Mr Reynolds, Nurse,' she said sharply, implying her no-nonsense attitude to juniors who wasted valuable time in unnecessary chit-chat with the patients.

'Mr Willis is feeling just a little anxious, staff,' Patti explained. 'I've just been telling him that he has nothing to worry about.'

The staff nurse seemed to bridle. 'You are in excellent hands, Mr Willis,' she said, very brisk. 'Mr Manning is a brilliant surgeon and knows just what he's doing—and I know that Mr Lewis spent a long time explaining everything to you last night.' There was a hint of reproach in her tone. 'You do want to get better, don't you, dear? That leg is no good to you as it is!'

The little man was too timid to protest, to declare that he had changed his mind and wanted to keep his leg, good or bad, but Patti saw the rising panic in the faded blue eyes and felt the frantic grip of the thin fingers.

Jenefer Neal bent over the bed with her bright, professional smile, hypodermic in hand. 'Just a small prick and then I want you to lie quietly and relax. Just leave everything to the doctors . . .'

Patti knew it was necessary to be firm. Pre-meds had to be given in good time and patients did tend to panic as the time drew near for them to go to Theatres. But the staff nurse seemed to look upon the elderly and naturally apprehensive patients as if they were difficult children.

The staff nurse straightened, dropped the syringe into the kidney dish. 'There we are, dear. Didn't hurt at all, did it? You'll be going up very shortly and soon it will be over and you can look forward to going home . . .' She went away with a last-minute admonition to Patti that Mr Reynolds was waiting for attention.

The old man looked after her with a hint of resentment. 'It's all right for her to be so blooming cheerful,' he muttered. 'It ain't her blooming leg . . .'

Patti understood how he felt. A nurse had to jolly the patients, but never at the risk of seeming not to care. Losing a leg might be a very routine business to a nurse who dealt with a variety of surgical cases but it was a major disaster to the patient. She stayed until the pre-med began to take effect. Within a few minutes, his grip on her hand relaxed and he eased himself more comfortably on the pillows. Then she left him to attend to the post-operative Mr Reynolds whose ruptured spinal discs had been removed two days before.

When she returned to Mr Willis some time later, he was in the slightly euphoric frame of mind that preceded drowsiness.

He gave her a toothless grin. 'Don't forget what you promised, Nurse,' he lisped. 'I want you down there with me . . .'

Patti smiled and promised and went to ask Sister if she could accompany him when the porters came to take him to Theatres.

Sister was in her office, talking earnestly to the anxious wife of a new patient. So she went to find Jenefer Neal, not very hopefully.

The staff nurse frowned. 'I've already told Nurse Long to go with Mr Willis. We've two more new admissions on their way up and I shall want you to look after them, Nurse.'

She was just being bloody-minded, Patti knew. There was no earthly reason why the other junior from her set should not attend to the new patients. But there was little point in arguing. The staff nurse was determined to be difficult. Well, she would just have to take the law into her own hands, she thought rebelliously. A promise was a promise.

Fortunately, Jenefer Neal was in a side ward when the porters arrived with the trolley and Madeleine Long was quite happy to relinquish her place to Patti. She did not even question the change of jobs.

The old man was sleepy but aware of her as she walked by the side of the trolley, clasping his folder to her breast, smiling and chatting and occasionally reaching to pat his shoulder as he was wheeled along the corridors to the waiting lift.

The anaesthetist and Mr Manning's assistant registrar were waiting in one of the ante-rooms to receive him.

It was difficult for Patti to reconcile the tall and strangely aloof figure, gowned and booted in readiness to assist at the operation, with the man who had held and kissed her with such passion. Ivor Maynard's dark hair was concealed beneath the green surgical cap. His mask had been pulled down for the benefit of the patient. The dark eyes glanced at her without any flicker of recognition or interest. He was more concerned with the patient than the accompanying nurse, of course.

Patti did not approve of the foolish flutter of her heart at sight of him or the little pang of disappointment when he turned away so indifferently. He bent over the trolley, spoke clearly and reassuringly to the drifting Mr Willis as the anaesthetist approached with poised hypodermic.

No time was wasted before Mr Willis was being wheeled into the antiseptic theatre where staff and instruments were waiting for the skilled surgeon to begin the operation. Patti caught just a glimpse of Oliver Manning before the doors swung to.

There was no reason for her to linger on the top floor. Sister would be notified when Mr Willis was sufficiently recovered to be returned to Currie and the nursing care of the ward staff. Patti sent up a silent prayer for his well-being and made her way back to the ward where Jenefer Neal waited for her, furious.

'Where have you been?' she demanded icily, knowing very well, suspecting that the junior had seized an opportunity to visit Theatres in the hope of a word with Ivor Maynard. Jenefer knew that they had been together on the previous evening and she was jealous and resentful, terribly afraid that she had made a fool of herself over yet another man.

'Taking Mr Willis to Theatres, Staff.'

Jenefer drew in her breath, sharply. 'Didn't I tell you to admit the new patients?'

'Yes, Staff.'

'Then perhaps you would like to explain why Nurse Long has been doing your work?'

Patti caught back a sigh. 'I asked her to swop jobs. She didn't mind and I didn't see that it mattered so much,' she said carefully.

The staff nurse glowered. 'Either Sister or myself decides who will do what on this ward, Nurse Parkin. Where would we be if all the staff swopped jobs to suit themselves? You are here to do as you are told and not to pander to the whims of patients!'

A little flush of anger rose in Patti's cheeks but she tightened the rein on her temper. 'He's an old man and he's frightened and he wanted me with him,' she said quietly. 'He looks on me as *his* nurse. You know the way that some patients take a fancy to a particular nurse. I just *couldn't* let him down.'

'It seems to me that you can't do anything you are told without argument or thinking that you know better than anyone else,' Jenefer said coldly. 'Obedience is one of the first essentials for a nurse. I'm afraid you'll never be a nurse worthy of the name, Nurse Parkin! I've had to report you to Sister, of course.'

'Of course,' Patti agreed, very dry.

Jenefer looked at her coldly, with dislike. The bright curls and the mocking green eyes and that pretty face might be very attractive to worthless men like Ivor Maynard. Jenefer was beginning to feel that she hated the girl who owned them. Certainly her fingers itched to slap her at that moment.

She checked the impulse. A hospital ward with its interested and observant patients was no place for a personal vendetta, she reminded herself firmly.

'She wants to see you in her office right away. You will be fortunate if she decides against sending you to Matron.' Her lips tightened. '*I* wouldn't hesitate!'

Patti didn't doubt it. The sharp-tongued senior was determined not to like her or to make the smallest allowance for her on the ward or off it. Sometimes she felt that her mop of hair was like a red rag to a bull where Jenefer Neal was concerned. But if rumour was to be believed, the staff nurse now had even more reason to resent her very existence—or thought she had, Patti amended swiftly, reminding herself that the association with Ivor Maynard was already at an end. Jenefer Neal could have him if that was what she wanted!

CHAPTER SEVEN

PATTI tugged at her apron and hoped her cap was in place. Then she tapped lightly on the office door, her heart pounding.

Sister Ann Percival was standing at the window that overlooked the ward, contemplating the neat rows of beds bathed in bright rays of sunshine that fell through the tall windows. She turned as Patti entered and looked at the first-year nurse for a long, expressive moment.

'Oh, dear . . .' she sighed ruefully.

Patti stood with hands demurely folded behind her back, a picture of innocence. She was genuinely sorry to be taking up Sister's valuable time with something so trivial. She knew that the older woman would have given permission and approval in the circumstances and only wished that she had waited to snatch a moment to ask for it instead of approaching the staff nurse.

Having nothing to say, she merely did her best to look contrite. As she could not regret keeping a promise, and as her eyes still held a faintly militant sparkle from that exchange with Jenefer Neal, it was not too easy.

Ann Percival surveyed the slight figure with the rebellious red hair. 'I should put your name on Matron's report, Nurse,' she said quietly.

'Yes, Sister.'

'Nurse Neal is the senior staff nurse on my ward, my second in command. When you disobey her instructions you are effectively disobeying me. A nurse must do as she is told without protest or question. A moment of rebellion or even hesitation at the wrong time could cost a patient's life. You do realise that, don't you, Nurse?'

'Yes, Sister. I'm very sorry, Sister.' That gentle tone was more effective than any scolding. Patti was reduced to the status of a schoolgirl whose behaviour had threatened the honour of the school. She felt that she must make some effort to vindicate herself. 'I should like to explain . . .'

'I know what you did and just why you did it. But that doesn't excuse the deliberate defiance of Nurse Neal's instructions, you know.' Sister was kindly but firm. 'I am suspending you from duty for the rest of the day. You may leave the ward immediately and report to me first thing in the morning.'

'But we're short-staffed, Sister . . .' The protest was instinctive, involuntary.

Sister Percival smiled wryly. 'Which makes it all the more necessary for everyone to get on with their work without these little upsets. We shall just have to manage without you, Nurse. Off you go!'

Patti bit her lip. 'Yes, Sister. Thank you, Sister.' She had got off very lightly, she knew. But she was dismayed. She had promised Mr Willis that she would be at his bedside when he came round in the ward. Some people might not regard it as a punishment to be sent home early from the day's work, but Patti felt it very keenly. She felt that she was letting down Sister and the rest of the ward staff and the patients.

She was not concerned with the comments of her fellow-nurses, sympathetic or otherwise. She was certainly not the first junior to be sent off a ward for breaking rules or flying in the face of tradition.

She was not concerned with the money that she would lose from her salary for the hours she did not work. She had not come into nursing with any thought of money, which was just as well for they were very poorly paid in comparison with outside jobs.

She was not particularly concerned with the fact that the day's suspension would be entered in her file, although it mattered very much that she should not earn any black marks during her training.

Patti *was* concerned with keeping her word to Mr Willis. It really hurt that hers would not be the first face he saw, the first voice he heard, when he roused from the drug-induced sleep that followed major surgery. Perhaps he would be too ill, too shocked, for it to matter to him. It mattered to Patti.

No doubt the shrewd and experienced Sister Percival knew that very well. She had known what she was about when she sent her from the ward with the instruction not to return until the following morning, Patti thought ruefully, taking off her apron in the juniors' room. Sister realised that such a salutary lesson would not be soon forgotten. It was unlikely that she would make that kind of promise to a patient so lightly in the future. A nurse never knew where she might be or what she might be doing at any given time and it had been foolish for Patti to assume that she would be free to hover about the ward until Mr Willis came round fully from the anaesthetic.

It was also unlikely that she would ignore an instruction so readily again, she thought wryly. She reminded herself firmly that she did not have to like Jenefer Neal to accept her authority as a senior nurse.

Leaving the ward, Patti went down the stone stairs to the ground floor and Main Hall. At this time of the day there was a constant stream of people coming and going through the swing doors and Jimmy, much occupied with answering queries and giving directions, had no time to notice one nurse among the many from his vantage point behind the big desk.

The Accident and Emergency Department just beyond Main Hall was particularly busy and Patti only managed to get a brief glimpse of Kate, her flatmate. She came out of one of the cubicles with a tiny but vociferous infant in her arms and sped with him towards a waiting incubator. One glance told Patti that the baby had only just arrived in the world, probably premature, and it was obvious that the mother had left it almost too late to seek medical help.

She pushed through the exit doors that led to the hospital garden and access to a variety of other hospital buildings. It was such a lovely day that she was tempted to sit in the bright sun for a little while. She ought to spend the rest of the day with her textbooks to make up for two evenings away from them—that would be sufficient penance for being sent off the ward, she thought. But first she would enjoy half an hour in the garden while she had the opportunity.

She sat down on one of the wooden seats that circled the statue of Sir Henry in the middle of the garden and looked with appreciation at the array of bright flowers and the verdant green of the well-kept lawns.

Some of the wards overlooked the garden and it was a cheerful, pleasant prospect for those patients whose beds were close to the windows. The garden was always a-bustle with people and there was much to be seen from where Patti sat. She watched the brisk, efficient progress of nurses about the wards and the slower, not too sure walk of convalescent patients. She could see into one of the clinical laboratories with its highly-skilled staff bent over the benches and the test-tubes.

The Preliminary Training School was just across the way. From where Patti sat, she could look into one of the lecture rooms and see the rows of attentive Pets, as they were called by the medical students, girls straight from school in many cases and as green as she had been only a few short months before. She could see Sister Tutor very clearly. The vivacious, dark-haired and dynamic Physiology Tutor knew just how to capture and hold the attention and interest of a group of girls who had to assimilate a number of facts in a very short time.

Much of nursing had to do with teaching, Patti had found. The first maxim of training was that one watched to learn how to carry out a task, then assisted while being supervised and then taught others. Even a first year like herself might be called upon to show a Pet, straight from PTS, how to lay up a trolley or change a dressing or check a drip. She might have learned it all in the classroom, but Patti knew from experience that the first few days on the wards were so fraught that one forgot almost everything learned in PTS. Theory might be very necessary, but practice on the wards really hammered it home.

Very few nurses had time to sit and stare. Patti attracted a good deal of attention and had to put up with the good-natured badinage of a group of medical students as well as curious stares from a number of ancillary staff. It was very pleasant to bask in the sun and rest her feet, even if she did feel guilty about not being at work on the ward.

She tried very hard not to think about Ivor Maynard. She thought about Mr Willis instead, and hoped he would not be too shocked after surgery and would make a good recovery—and wondered how that brought her round to thinking of Ivor again. That brief encounter in Theatres, of course . . .

She had merited no more than a glance. Certainly there had not even been the flicker of a smile in those dark eyes. He had been so intent on his patient that she wondered if he had even seen her. A nurse was just a faceless robot to many of the doctors, but it scarcely seemed likely that he could have overlooked her flaming hair.

It was that flaming hair that caught the eye of a

man who paused just by the swing doors that led to Out-Patients. Steve looked—and looked again with satisfaction and relief. He had not really expected to find her so easily in the big, rambling hospital with its many wards and departments and its labyrinth of corridors. He had discovered that she was on duty and he knew the ward on which she was currently working. Realising that he could not invade the ward in search of her, he had decided to have a look around the famous hospital.

He gazed at the slight figure in the print frock sitting on the wooden seat, hands folded quietly in her lap. She looked like a good little girl playing at doctors and nurses, Steve thought, amused. Then he saw that she was too still, too grave. He frowned. All her letters home declared that she was happy at Hartlake. He did not think that she could be happy. She looked tired and a little lost. His heart smote him suddenly. He began to walk across the lawn towards her, swiftly.

Patti glanced idly at the approaching figure. Then her heart lurched in disbelieving delight. *Steve!* Fair and stocky and boyishly handsome, with that slightly rueful smile about his lips that had always caught at her heart. Walking towards her with the old, familiar eagerness in his stride as though nothing had changed, as though he had not shattered all her hopes and dreams by marrying her cousin.

'Steve!' She said his name on a surge of warm delight, eyes wide as though she did not believe he could be there in the flesh when he belonged only in her dreams these days.

He smiled down at her, confident. The way she looked, colour leaping into her pretty face, and the way she said his name told him that she still loved him.

'Hallo, Patience,' he said quietly and sat down beside her on the seat.

It was ages since anyone had used her full name. She was Patti to everyone at Hartlake and that was how she liked it. She did not feel like Patience any more, in fact. She had lived up to that name only too well where Steve was concerned, and it had gained her nothing. She could not help feeling just a little spurt of resentment that he should greet her as if nothing had happened to ruin their relationship. It marred all her pleasure at seeing him.

'What on earth are you doing here?' Lancaster seemed a million miles from Hartlake at times. She suddenly touched his hand, anxious. 'You aren't ill?' Her voice was concerned.

He took her hand in both his own. 'No, I'm fine. I wanted to see you.' The directness of the words, the warmth in his eyes, threw her off balance.

'You look well,' she said, and thought how absurd it was to utter inane platitudes to a man who had been so dear to her for so long. But this unexpected meeting was not in the least how she had dreamed it, again and again, never believing that it could come true and that he might really come to her one day and admit that he had been wrong and that he loved her still.

'I *am* well.' He was brusque, slightly impatient.

'And . . . Valerie?' She forced herself to speak her cousin's name as lightly as she could.

He winced. 'We won't talk about Val,' he said involuntarily.

Patti was silent as he gently stroked the soft, velvety flesh of her wrist in the unconscious habit that convinced her that it really was Steve at her side and not just a figment of her imagination.

'Aren't you happy?' she asked quietly, carefully, torn between pain for him and a very natural wish to believe that it was impossible for him to find happiness with anyone but herself. 'Isn't it working out?'

'It's a bloody disaster,' he said bluntly.

'Oh, darling!' she exclaimed in genuine dismay, the endearment flowing from her lips on a tide of remembered loving. 'I'm so sorry . . . !'

He shrugged. 'My own fault. I must have been mad, I think. I miss you terribly—all the time.' The words came out jerkily. He had rehearsed all the things he would say to her. He had certainly not meant to blurt out the misery of his marriage in the first few moments. But she was so sweet, so pretty, so warmly concerned for him and he had realised all in a rush just what he had thrown away for the sake of an impulsive and short-lived infatuation.

Patti bit her lip, but said nothing. What could she say? *I told you so* might tremble on her lips, but she was not the kind of girl to rub salt into the wound.

Surprisingly, she felt for Valerie. Her cousin had tumbled headlong into love and Patti was sure that it had been genuine. Valerie had been distressed by the thought of coming between them, but driven by the force of her feelings. And Steve had seemed to be just as much in love, Patti thought, remembering with an echo of pain that only her conviction on that score had made it possible for her to accept, to wish them happy, to pretend that it was not tearing her to pieces to lose him.

She was shocked that the marriage semed to have broken down so soon. She wondered if Steve, naturally impatient and inclined to expect too much from everyone and everything, had really given it a chance. Had he fallen out of love so quickly? Or had he never really loved Valerie at all?

He looked and spoke now as if he still loved *her*, Patti thought, but it was ashes in her mouth, the dust of a dream. For they could not take their happiness at Valerie's expense. Patti could not believe that someone as consistent and as conscientious as her cousin had ceased to care and Steve freely admitted that he was to blame for the breakdown. Knowing him, Patti did not doubt it. Loving him, she had never been blind to his faults.

In love with Valerie, he must have been a devoted and considerate and caring husband. Out of love, feeling cheated and knowing that he had trapped himself through impulse, he must have been hell. Poor Valerie . . .

'What are you doing in London?' Patti asked, drawing her hand from his clasp, discovering that the persistent little caress of his thumb was an irritation. 'Surely you haven't come all this way just to see me?'

'I arranged a transfer to the London office. Better prospects, more money—and I couldn't take any more of Lancaster, without you. We've given up the flat. Val's gone home to mother,' he added, faintly mocking.

Patti looked at him, troubled. 'That sounds very final.'

'It is final. We were just making each other miserable.' He smiled, very wry. 'It's a mess, Patience. All it needs is for you to say that you don't love me any more and I might as well throw myself under a bus.'

Patti knew how little he meant the threat. Steve would never take anything that seriously. He was an incurable optimist. Everything would always come right in the end—and if it didn't then it would be anyone's fault but his own. So it had surprised her that he was so ready to admit blame for the failure of his marriage.

'You'd probably make a hash of that and I'd have to nurse you back to health,' she said. But the warm affection in her eyes belied the stringent words.

He laughed. 'I believe you would, too,' he said warmly. 'You're so generous, Patience. That's only one of the reasons why I love you. I do, you know.' His voice softened. 'I've always loved you. I've just been a fool.' He sighed, brightened instantly. 'But that's all behind us, darling. Val understands. She isn't happy about it, but she won't make waves.'

Patti's heart seemed to stop with the shock of the words and their unmistakable meaning. She felt breathless, a little sick. Things were happening too quickly. Only a few minutes before, she had believed him to be in Lancaster, happily married, and herself to be near to forgetting the heartbreak he had caused. Now, he was at her side, smiling into her eyes with all the boyish, heart-wrenching charm of old and the confident assurance that she had used to admire so much, but which now seemed just a little brash.

He was too full of himself and too sure of her. The disloyal thought came swiftly, surprising and dismaying her. She thrust it aside. She loved him. After all, he loved her. She should be the happiest girl in the world at that moment.

Instead, her heart was heavy. He had overlooked her strict upbringing, her instinctive dislike of coming between a man and his wife. It might be an old-fashioned point of view in these permissive days when marriage was entered into so lightly and divorce was commonplace, but Patti did not like the breaking of vows before the ink was dry on the marriage register. She could not fall into his arms with glad cries of delight and forget that Valerie existed, as he seemed to expect. Not yet, anyway—not until she had come to terms with his unexpected invasion of her new life at Hartlake.

She rose to her feet. 'I don't know what to say to you, Steve,' she said slowly. 'I don't know what you expect from me. Everything's changed . . .'

He was suddenly tense. He caught her arm, his hand tightening so fiercely that she knew his strong fingers would leave marks on the flesh. 'You've changed, do you mean? *Have* you stopped loving me—found someone else? I don't think I could bear that!'

Moved by the very real apprehension in his eyes, the intensity of his tone, Patti smiled in swift reassurance and impulsively touched her hand to his cheek. 'No! How could I?' Loving him had been the most important thing in her life for years. She did not believe that such loving could come to an end. Of course she loved him still!

Triumphant, Steve put both arms about her and kissed her soundly, in full view of anyone who cared to glance at the couple who stood beneath the statue of the hospital's founder. Sir Henry looked down on them benevolently. He had been a warm-hearted philanthropist and he had seen it all before from his plinth in the last eighty years.

The colour was a fierce banner in Patti's cheeks as she pulled away, too embarrassed to have found the slightest satisfaction or pleasure in that embrace. For months, she had longed to know his arms about her again, his warm and tender kiss, his surging need of her—and believed it to be a hopeless dream. Now that it had come true, time and place were so wrong that she was filled with painful dismay.

'Steve! I'm wearing my uniform!' she exclaimed, horrified. She had broken a strict hospital rule. Nurses were not regarded as human beings with a personal life of their own when they were in the hospital precincts. On or off duty, if they were in uniform they had to be discreet and careful of their dignity. Nurses were the next thing to saints in the eyes of the public, after all—a hangover from the past when the only nurses were nuns, perhaps.

Steve raised an amused eyebrow. 'There's no law against kissing a pretty nurse—and you *are* very pretty in that absurd cap. I bet you're a wow with the patients. Working on a men's ward, aren't you?

The sour old bird at the Nurses' Home told me that much. I said I was your cousin. She wouldn't have given anything away if I hadn't—and it's more or less the truth, isn't it?'

Patti did not smile. It hurt that he could refer so casually, so cheerfully, to the circumstances that had made him more or less her cousin and had come close to breaking her heart.

'Hartlake has its own laws. Matron would be down on me like a ton of bricks if she'd seen us kissing . . . especially just here where we can be seen by half the hospital!'

'Do you care?' He grinned at her, very confident. 'You won't be here much longer, after all. I have much better plans for your future, darling.'

Patti was shaken by the calm assumption that she would agree to those plans as though she had no mind of her own—and suddenly she realised just how much she had changed in a few short months. Once, she would never have questioned his right to decide her future while it seemed that she would share it with him.

CHAPTER EIGHT

PATTI began to walk along the paved path towards the main hospital building, feeling that they were much too conspicuous where they stood. He fell into step beside her.

'I enjoy nursing, Steve,' she said quietly. 'I want to go on with my training. Nurses are so desperately needed . . . and it's such a worthwhile job.'

Impatience flashed in the blue eyes, but he thought he understood her resistance. The way he had treated her did not make her too ready to trust him again.

'You must do as you think best,' he said reasonably. 'But I need you more than a lot of sick strangers, sweetheart.'

Patti glanced at him, struck anew by the selfish streak that cared for little but his own concerns, his own wishes. She had always known it, but made allowance because she loved him. Now, suddenly, although she loved him still, she felt that she did not like him very much.

Meeting those expressive green eyes, Steve felt faintly uncomfortable. He hastened to rectify that mistake. 'I know that sounds callous, but I've missed you so much. I don't want to share you with anyone. I love you! I want you to come and live with me. As soon as I can get a divorce, we'll be married. Darling, I won't let you down again. Trust me!'

'I'm not allowed to live out as a first-year,' she

said, stretching the truth slightly.

'That settles it, then. You'll *have* to give up nursing.'

She stopped short. 'You're asking an awful lot of me, Steve,' she told him bluntly.

'Too much?' he returned promptly, with just a touch of reproach. 'I thought you loved me, Patience.'

She sighed. 'You know I do.' Her eyes sparked suddenly. 'And that's blackmail of the worst possible kind!'

He laughed, unrepentant. 'I know it is! I'll stoop to anything. Darling, you can't possibly want to be stuck in this place, working your fingers to the bone for a mere pittance, when I'm on the other side of London. We shall hardly see each other. I know the kind of hours a nurse works and it's ridiculous!'

'I don't want to leave Hartlake,' she said, stubborn.

He capitulated. 'All right. It's your life. I've no right to ask anything of you while I'm still married to Val. I shouldn't have come here to see you. It isn't fair to either of us.'

Patti looked at him doubtfully. He sounded sincere, but she suspected it was more blackmail, differently phrased.

'You know how glad I am to see you,' she said quietly. 'I love you, Steve. *I* haven't changed. I'd still do anything to please you, make you happy . . .'

'Except live with me.' He was brusque.

She put her hand on his arm. 'You must give me a little time to think about it. Ten minutes ago, I didn't even know you were in London!'

'Ten minutes ago, I didn't mean to rush you into

anything. I don't think I realised just how much I love you, just how important you are, until I saw you on that seat, looking so forlorn.'

'Forlorn!' Patti was a trifle indignant. 'I was enjoying the sunshine and feeling perfectly content!' She walked on, mounting the few steps to the entrance doors.

He followed her. 'And not even thinking about me,' he said wryly, opening the doors for her to pass through.

'Not just then.'

'Not at all these days, perhaps.'

Patti hesitated. Then she said honestly: 'Sometimes I've wished I could put you out of my mind, Steve. I might have been happier all these months. But my life revolved about you for so long that it just wasn't possible.'

He reached for her hand, pressed it. 'I'm glad.'

As they passed the open doors of Accident and Emergency, Kate saw her, waved. Patti smiled at her friend. 'My flatmate,' she explained to Steve. 'I share a flat with Kate and two other girls in the Nurses' Home. We're not allowed to entertain men-friends in the flats, of course. But there is a communal lounge where we can talk. I'm off duty for the rest of the day.'

'Really!' He brightened. 'Then I chose the right day to come looking for you, sweetheart. You can change into something pretty and get away from these grim surroundings for a few hours. I've got my car. I'll take you to see the flat I've found in Richmond. It's expensive but worth every penny, darling . . . and when you've seen it, you might just feel that you could bear to share it with me,' he added lightly.

Patti felt apprehensive, oddly reluctant. She ought not to object to the idea of going to his flat. She realised that he was hoping to make love to her, bind her to him once more with the lasting ties of passion—and it was rather late in the day to turn prudish where he was concerned. They had been lovers for a long time before he met and married Valerie. She did not think that Steve would understand her scruples. But while their love for each other had made the sexual relationship both right and natural in the past, he was now another woman's husband. Patti did not feel that she could lightly betray her cousin or her own principles by encouraging him to commit adultery.

She was a very honest person. She squarely faced the unpalatable fact that she might not be so scrupulous if her body responded to Steve as passionately as it did to Ivor Maynard. Instinct might be more overwhelming than principle when the sexual urge was that strong, she felt. As it was, Steve did not excite her, stir her senses, urge her to forget everything in his arms.

She might allow herself to be persuaded into lovemaking because she cared enough for him to overcome that initial distaste. But it would not be because she wanted him too much to resist temptation.

'You mustn't assume that I've nothing else to do with my day, Steve,' she said, in light but meaningful reproach. 'I didn't know I'd be seeing you, after all. I might have other plans.'

'And have you?' His smile implied that he knew she was merely making a stand, asserting her independence.

'Nothing very important. But I don't want to go too far from the hospital.' She was suddenly inspired by the realisation that while she could not return to the ward in her rôle as a nurse, she must be able to see Mr Willis as a visitor! 'I promised to see a friend on one of the wards. I mustn't let him down.'

Steve frowned. 'Boyfriend?' His tone was sharp.

Patti smiled, a little mischievously. 'I'm very fond of him,' she agreed, amused. 'And he seems to have taken a fancy to me.' Seeing a flicker of anxiety in his blue eyes, she hastened to explain. 'He's a patient—a dear old man of seventy-odd. He's in Theatres right now, having a leg amputated. I must go up to the ward to see him later this afternoon.'

'You can see him tomorrow, darling,' he protested. 'You can't want to ruin an entire day for the sake of an old man who won't even know you're there! He's bound to be dopey from the anaesthetic.'

'I must see him, Steve,' Patti repeated, firmly.

He shrugged. 'Oh, if you insist . . .'

She had become very stubborn, he decided. Once, she had been willing to be guided by him, to accept his word as the final authority on most things. It scarcely seemed that she could be the same girl who had always been so eager to please him. She claimed that she had not changed. She was wrong. Nursing had changed her, she had lost some of her warmth and sweetness. She was becoming hard and much too independent . . .

Patti left him in the lounge with a newspaper

while she hurried up to the flat to change out of her uniform. She was glad to have a few minutes to herself. She needed to draw a deep breath, to take stock, to pinch herself to make sure that it wasn't all just another dream.

He was so much a part of her life, her background, that there had seemed nothing unusual in walking with him, talking to him, for all the months between that he had spent with Valerie. She was naturally at ease with him. He was not only her love. They had been friends for a very long time and they had many good times to recall, many things in common, many memories to share.

She was glad to see him. She was a little sad, too. Everything would have been so different if he had not believed himself in love with Valerie and rushed into marriage. She could not help feeling just a little bitter—and just a little angry with him. He had held back from marrying her for a variety of reasons that Patti had always been reluctant to describe as excuses, and she had been patient and trusting because she loved him. The urgency of his desire to marry her cousin had seemed like a slap in the face, positive proof that he had never really loved her in truth. She had felt used and it still rankled.

She almost wished that she no longer loved him. It would be only his just deserts if she turned her back on him after the way he had treated her. But she did love him and her tender heart would not allow her to seek the smallest revenge for past hurt and humiliation. At the same time, she did not feel as ready as he seemed to believe to forget and forgive and fall into his arms. It would take a little time to think well of him again. Loving was all very well, but liking and respect were equally important, it seemed to Patti . . . and he would need to earn those all over again.

He took her to lunch at an expensive restaurant and talked a great deal about himself, his prospects in the new job, his hopes and plans for the future. Patti was used to listening while he expounded at length and she was a good listener. She was genuinely interested, too. His future might well be her own, after all. But she did not mean to give up nursing and move into his flat with him at the lift of a finger.

He was not very interested in Hartlake. As far as he was concerned, nursing had provided her with an interest and an outlet while he came to his senses. Now, it was no longer necessary for her to concentrate on anything but him and the life they would make together.

Patti disagreed. She had discovered that there was more to life than devoting it entirely to one person. She would never again look upon marriage as the only career for a woman. She had taken to nursing like a duck to water and she wanted to finish her training. She wanted to carry on nursing even if she married Steve. It was something he would have to accept. For the first time she felt that she was in a position to exercise her own rights as a person.

Her attitudes and ideas had altered. Love and marriage no longer seemed the be-all and end-all of everything in life. She had discovered that there could be fulfilment in other things, such as a worthwhile and rewarding job in a busy hospital.

She did not tell him so. There would be plenty of

time to put over her point of view for she was determined not to be rushed into anything. Patti decided that she could be very determined these days.

After lunch, they made their way to the Tower of London and wandered about the grounds and admired the battlements, hand in hand like lovers. Patti's bright hair and sparkling prettiness and shapely figure in the silk suit attracted attention and admiring glances from other visitors. That pleased Steve. He liked to be seen in the company of a pretty and personable girl, liked to feel that other men envied him his companion.

Val was tall and slim and fashionably elegant and she had very expensive tastes in clothes and jewellery. She had style and a glittering charm that had bowled him over, swept him into marriage. But she had proved to be critical, demanding, very possessive. Patience had never been any of those things, he remembered . . . and it had not taken him very long to feel that he had made a mistake.

Well, mistakes could be rectified. It might take a little time to obtain a divorce, but Patience would wait. He did not doubt that he could soon overcome her present reluctance to live with him in the meantime.

He set himself to charm, to please, to smoothe her still ruffled feathers. It was very important to convince Patience that he did love her and meant to marry her as soon as he was free to do so. Just now, she was not ready to trust him on either count, he realised . . .

Patti enjoyed the afternoon with Steve. It was so much like old times that she could almost forget that his marriage and her months at Hartlake had intervened. But she did not mean to forget Mr Willis and she kept a careful eye on the time. A little reluctantly, Steve agreed to drive her back to the hospital so that she could visit the old man. In return, she agreed to spend the evening with him at his flat in Richmond. She realised where that would lead them, but she was warming to him with every passing hour and perhaps their feeling for each other could excuse the fact that he was a married man . . .

Steve told her that he would wait in the car while she went up to the ward. Patti leaned to brush his cheek with her lips on a surge of affection. 'I won't be very long,' she assured him, confident that Mr Willis would be round from the anaesthetic and back on the ward by this time. She hoped that no other nurse on the ward had yet roused him and that he would stir from sleep at her touch on his shoulder.

She slipped into the ward. It was still afternoon visiting hours and many of the staff were taking advantage of a brief lull in the busy day. There was no sign of Sister Percival. Patti kept a wary eye out for Jenefer Neal.

Marian Foster saw her from a side ward where she was adjusting the drip of a patient newly back from Theatres. She raised her eyebrows. Patti put her finger to her lips. Marian smiled, left the patient and came to the door to speak to her.

'What are you doing on the ward? You were suspended, weren't you?'

Patti groaned. 'I suppose the entire hospital has heard about it,' she said ruefully. 'I want to see Mr

Willis. Is he back from Theatres? Where is everyone?'

'Everyone being Sister and Staff Nurse Neal,' Marian suggested, smiling. 'Sister is in her sitting-room, enjoying a much-needed cup of tea. I'm not sure about Neal. She was on the ward only a few minutes ago. Mr Willis is in his own bed, curtains drawn. Make it a very quick visit, Patti.'

'How is he?'

Marian shook her head. 'Not good.'

Patti made her way through the ward to the screened bed, smiling at one or two patients who did not immediately recognise her out of uniform. Wearing the soft green suit that brought out the green in her eyes, and matching high-heeled shoes, she supposed that she looked like just another visitor to them.

Mr Willis was not allowed any visitors that day, as was usual after surgery. If there was anxiety about his condition, his relatives would be informed and he would be moved into a side ward and his name entered on the seriously-ill list and the rules about visiting relaxed. Despite Marian's gloom, it seemed that he was expected to make satisfactory progress as he had been returned to his own bed in the ward.

Patti slipped behind the curtains. He was sleeping off the effects of the anaesthetic. The little man seemed to melt into the pillow and the huge mound of the cradle that protected him from the weight of the bedclothes seemed incongruous by comparison. His face was waxy and sunken and his breathing was stertorous. He looked very old and very ill, but Patti knew how rapidly his colour and breathing could improve and how miraculously the body could combat even major surgery with the aid of modern drugs and antibiotics.

A cylinder of oxygen stood beside the bed in case of need. A drip kept up a steady flow of saline into the vein. Looking at his chart, Patti saw that his pulse was erratic and the blood pressure was low. But he was under half-hourly observation and there really should not be anything for her to worry about.

Yet, looking down at him, Patti found her eyes filling with tears. Nurses were not supposed to become emotionally involved with patients, but she had grown fond of the little man and she really cared that he should get well. She did not think he would and could not explain the feeling even to herself.

She put her hand on his shoulder, said his name gently. He mumbled something indistinguishable. 'Mr Willis,' she called again, 'how are you?' The rheumy old eyes fluttered, opened, looked at her vacantly. She smiled . . . and the bright warmth of her smile penetrated his drowsy state of mind like a shaft of sunshine.

'That you, gel . . . ?'

Patti could only just make out the words. 'I just came to see how you are, Mr Willis,' she said clearly, patting his shoulder. 'Don't wake up . . .'

'. . . hair of yourn—like my Lil's before . . . it faded. White she was—at the last . . .' The words rose and fell in gusts of breathless effort. He was still and Patti began to think he'd drifted into sleep again. Then he stirred. 'Flaming ginger when . . . I married 'er. Lovely, she was . . .' His voice trailed away.

Patti waited a few moments. Then, satisfied that he slept and glad that she had kept her word to him, she slipped through the curtains and mingled with the departing visitors, hoping that Sister would not notice her conspicuously bright hair as she passed her, talking to one of the housemen by the desk.

In the corridor, she almost ran into Jenefer Neal. The sound of her voice preceded the staff nurse before she turned the corner. Patti hastily opened the door of the spacious linen cupboard and stepped inside, almost but not quite closing the door. She listened to the footsteps approaching, pausing. She recognised the second voice but could not catch the words it spoke. The footsteps passed the door. After a moment, she ventured to push open the door slightly to glance out into the corridor.

Ivor stood talking to Jenefer Neal by the swing doors of the ward. She had tickets for a show at the Palladium and had asked him to go with her if he was free. He saw no reason to refuse. He was still smarting slightly from Patti's rebuff and knew from past experience that the best cure for that kind of hurt was the company of another woman.

Jenefer was attractive and amusing and he liked her well enough—and a little attention from him might make her less hard on a certain copper-haired junior, he thought, having heard rumours that she disliked his obvious interest in Patti and was giving the girl a bad time on the ward.

The staff nurse had her back to the linen cupboard. Ivor saw the door open and close again with suspicious haste and just caught a glimpse of green. Amusement flickered in his dark eyes. He knew some of the things that went on in linen cupboards, having indulged in some of them himself through the years. No doubt one of the juniors was enjoying a crafty cuddle with a medical student. But that flicker of green puzzled him. No one at Hartlake wore green except the surgical teams and this had been a much softer shade. Maybe a visitor had opened the door and walked in, mistaking a cupboard for something totally different, and was now too embarrassed to emerge until the coast was clear.

Parting with Jenefer, he deliberately raised his voice so that the occupant of the roomy cupboard would know that they were going their separate ways. As the staff nurse pushed through the swing doors of the ward, Patti thankfully left the cupboard.

He had not expected it to be Patti. He quickened at sight of that pretty face and shining hair. Her eyes were rueful as she looked at him. He moved towards her, a little smile in his dark eyes. 'Hide and seek, is it?' he drawled, teasing. 'Can anyone play?'

Even as he spoke, Jenefer Neal appeared at the door of the ward again, fortunately looking over her shoulder as she spoke to someone behind her.

'Don't give me away!' Patti said urgently.

In a moment, Ivor had caught her arm and thrust her into the cupboard and pulled the door shut on them both with such a conspiratorial air that Patti began to giggle.

'She'll think you vanished into thin air!' she exclaimed, chuckling.

'Ssh!' he cautioned, dark eyes dancing.

Patti could not stop laughing as she imagined the staff nurse's bewildered expression as she looked for the registrar ... there one moment, gone the next! She had never known anyone to react so rapidly. He was a very quick thinker—or else he was very practised in whisking nurses out of sight when authority loomed into view!

Ivor looked down at her, amused. 'Idiot girl,' he said softly, and the epithet sounded like an endearment. 'Why are you hiding in a cupboard?'

'I'm in disgrace. I'm not supposed to be on the ward.' She explained quickly, sobered.

'Mr Willis? Friend of yours, is he?'

She nodded. 'He's such a sweet old man. I hope he's going to be all right. He doesn't seem very well.'

'He'll be fine,' Ivor said reassuringly. 'There were no complications and he came through surgery well. My boss is pleased with him. These old Cockneys are as tough as boot leather, you know, Patti. By this time tomorrow, he'll be sitting up and taking notice. You'll see.'

'Yes. I expect you're right.' Patti wanted to believe him and he had a great deal of experience of such cases. 'Thanks ...' She smiled at him, warmly, gratefully.

There was a remembered glow in the dark eyes as she looked up at him. Patti's heart lurched and a tingling shivered along her spine and then he bent his head and laid his lips gently on her own.

Patti did not know how it happened that she was in his arms and returning his kiss with an eager abandon that turned the world topsy-turvy ...

CHAPTER NINE

SHE had not meant it to happen. She had not expected it to happen, even though it must have seemed a golden opportunity to a man with Ivor Maynard's reputation for making the most of such opportunities.

Patti clung to him, senses swimming. She could feel the thud of his heart against her soft breast, so tightly did he hold her. Her body was melting with the longing that his touch triggered, and it alarmed her that his body was so hard, so urgent, throbbing with passion. The desire that leaped between them was too fierce, too dangerous. It had its roots in nothing but sexual attraction, she reminded herself desperately.

Remembering Steve, who was waiting so patiently in his car for her return, Patti was shamed by her need for a man she could never love, a man whose wanting owed nothing to loving. She was shocked, too, by the intensity of that mutual need. Whatever had held him back before, she knew now that he wanted her just as certainly as she wanted him. It was a very dangerous flame.

She tried to draw away. His arms only tightened all the more fiercely. 'Please . . .' she said shakily.

Reluctantly, Ivor released her, fighting the turmoil of his senses. 'You're too much temptation, girl,' he said again softly, meaning it. She seemed to draw the very heart out of him. If it was not loving, it was still new to him, nothing like the way he had felt about women in the past.

She smiled, tremulous. 'I don't like what you do to me, either,' she said frankly. There was no point in trying to hide what her body betrayed only too plainly.

Amusement crinkled his eyes. 'Did I say that I didn't like it?'

He put his arm about her again. Patti pushed him away, resolute. 'Someone's waiting for me, Ivor . . . I must go!'

He glanced at his watch. 'I'm free in half an hour, Patti. We could have the rest of the day together.' His tone, his smile, were warmly persuasive. 'We'll go out for a meal, do a show, anything you like . . .'

'I can't. I told you, Ivor. Someone is waiting for me,' she said, a little reluctantly, knowing that she should tell him about Steve and hesitating to shatter their relationship completely.

His eyes were rueful. 'Is he important?' He knew it must be a man. She would have said quickly enough if it was a girl-friend. 'I have so little free time. It might be days before I can devote an entire evening to you.'

She understood his urgency. She caught back the disloyal thought that Steve might have chosen any day but this one to walk back into her life. She told herself firmly that Providence had probably saved her from doing something she would certainly regret. Sex without love was no part of her code for living, and no matter how they spent the evening it was inevitable that she would end up in bed with

Ivor Maynard if she went out with him again.

'I'm sorry . . .'

He nodded. 'I mustn't expect you to change your plans all in a moment to suit me, of course,' he agreed reasonably, but disappointment showed itself in his smile.

Patti put her hand to the door. 'Do you think the coast is clear?'

'Sister is probably waiting to catch us red-handed,' he warned lightly.

But there was no one about in the corridor. Patti breathed a sigh of relief and hurried towards the lift. Ivor followed.

He accompanied her down to the ground floor and across Main Hall. Patti wished he would not, but she could scarcely refuse to let him walk with her. It seemed to her that heads turned and voices whispered as they passed. He was so tall, so distinctive, so well-known—and her hair, suddenly the bane of her life, attracted too much notice wherever she went at Hartlake. Knowing that the Head Porter's gaze was on them as they crossed Main Hall, Patti carefully did not look in Jimmy's direction. She was sure he would send her a knowing wink and the smile that was his blessing on a new romance. There was no romance between herself and Ivor Maynard, she thought firmly—and wished she could put up a poster to that effect to stop the inevitable grapevine gossip!

They paused at the head of the steps that led down to the street from the main entrance of the hospital. Patti glanced involuntarily towards Steve's car, parked in a meter bay just a few yards along the High Street. Steve had left the car and was pacing the pavement impatiently, glancing every now and again at his watch. Catching sight of Patti and her companion, he checked and stared with sudden suspicion.

Ivor looked down at Patti's suddenly hot face. 'Your date?'

'Yes.' She hesitated and then she said involuntarily: 'We used to be engaged. I haven't seen him since I began my training.' She did not know what prompted the words. She had never spoken of Steve to anyone since coming to Hartlake. Perhaps she felt that she owed Ivor an explanation for keeping him at arms' length when he must know that she was not entirely indifferent to him. She had encouraged him too much, she admitted ruefully . . . and allowed herself to think about him far too much!

Ivor did not need to ask who had broken that engagement. It was the explanation for so much that had puzzled him about Patti. Hurt once, Patti did not mean to be hurt again, he suspected. He refused to accept that she could still be in love with the man who had let her down. She did not smile at him, kiss him, melt into his arms like a woman in love with someone else. She was not in love with him, either. But her heart was certainly her own whether she knew it or not. It seemed to Ivor that she might just be reluctant to admit that she could have had a change of heart about a man who had once been important to her. He had met that particular brand of pride in a woman before . . .

He did not react as though her words were of any

particular interest or importance to him. He merely nodded, smiled. 'See you around, Patti . . .' he said carelessly and turned to walk back into the hospital.

Patti ran down the steps and hurried to join Steve, thrusting the thought of Ivor Maynard to the back of her mind.

'How was the old boy?' Steve asked indifferently. Without waiting for her reply, he swept on: 'Hurry up and get in, Patience. I'm out of time and there's a traffic warden heading this way.'

They had covered several miles on their way to Richmond before he asked, a little abruptly: 'Who was the tall chap in the white coat?' He turned his head, smiling. 'Boyfriend?'

Patti wondered what kind of aura had surrounded them as she stood with Ivor at the top of the steps that Steve had sensed from a distance that there was something between them.

'No. One of the registrars. I don't know him very well.' It was the truth. There was no need to say more, no need for Steve to know the impact of another man's physical attractions on her startled senses.

Her hands were locked tightly in her lap. Steve recognised the sign of tension. He glanced at her curiously. 'You're tense. What's wrong?'

Patti *was* tense, all knotted up inside at the thought of the lovemaking to come. His kisses, his caresses, had never stirred her in the past. Would they now that her body knew how to respond to a man's nearness? Or was it only Ivor Maynard who could sweep her to the edge of ecstasy with that trembling passion in his embrace? She ought not to shrink from the thought of Steve's kiss, Steve's touch, Steve's demanding body that was used to taking its own satisfaction at the expense of hers. Patti suddenly realised, with a new awareness, his selfishness and immaturity.

'Thinking of Mr Willis,' she said and it wasn't quite a lie for the little man was still in the forefront of her mind. 'I'm anxious about him.'

Steve shook his head, smiling. 'He's just a patient, sweetheart. Forget him.' He reached to cover her hands with one of his own. 'Think about me, Patience—and how good it is to be together again.' With an eye on the traffic lights that had temporarily halted the car, he leaned to kiss her, brushing her lips lightly in the old, teasing, meaningful manner.

Patti smiled, touched his cheek. She loved him and it *was* good to be with him, she thought on a familiar surge of affection. Perhaps he was selfish, a little weak, inclined to be hasty and irresponsible and very much wrapped up in his own concerns, but that was the Steve she knew and still loved despite everything. Her feeling for him had not changed, could never change, she was sure. Ivor Maynard was just a fever in the blood, a temporary magic that had nothing to do with the reality that was her love for Steve . . .

The flat was at the top of a modern block halfway up Richmond's famous hill and the views from the windows were impressive, breathtaking. Patti loved it and said so, warmly.

Steve came to stand behind her and put his arms about her as she stood by the window. 'I knew you would, sweetheart. See the sun on the river as it winds into the country? And down towards the city? Magnificent, isn't it? Think of waking to that view every morning . . . with me by your side!' He nuzzled her neck.

She turned in his arms and smiled up at him. 'I'm tempted, I must admit,' she said lightly.

'By the view—or me?' He kissed her, light, undemanding. He had not the least doubt that he would get what he wanted. He always did.

Patti wished he did tempt her. There was not even a flicker of response in her to his embrace, his kiss. He did not realise, she knew. Steve had never been particularly sensitive to her moods.

After all, she did not have the heart to refuse him. He was loving, tender, persuasive—and shrewd enough to give her time to mellow. He loved her, he said. He had missed her. Valerie had been a terrible mistake and it had been hell all these months without her. They were meant for each other, he said . . . and Patti allowed herself to be swayed, allowed him to make love to her with the eager, swiftly satisfied passion that was so familiar.

Later, she lay in his arms and wondered why she was not content to have pleased him as in the past. His happiness, his delight, had always been more important to her than her own enjoyment of sex. Now, she found herself resenting his easy, untroubled acceptance of her lack of fulfilment.

Ivor would *care*, she thought with an odd pang. Her delight in such an encounter would be as important to him as his own. He would ensure her satisfaction or feel that he had failed her. But there was not the least doubt in Patti's mind or body that she could soar to the very heights of glorious ecstasy in Ivor's arms. It was how it should be with Steve whom she loved. Sadly, she knew in her heart that it never would be . . .

Steve wanted her to stay the night and could not understand her insistence that she must go back to the Nurses' Home. Nor did he understand how important it was that she should report for duty the next day.

'Take a few days off,' he urged. 'You look so tired. They're working you into the ground and I don't know why you like the job so much.' He shook his fair head in genuine bewilderment.

'I can't take time off just like that!' Patti exclaimed, horrified. 'We're short-staffed as it is and Currie is one of our busiest wards!'

'What if you were ill?'

'That would be different, of course. I'd be admitted to Sick Bay and receive the kind of expert attention and loving care that our patients get.' She smiled at him. 'Darling, I'm not ill and I do love my work and I really must go in.'

'And you mean to continue with this training nonsense?' His mouth set in a thin line of annoyance.

Patti stifled a little spark of anger. 'Yes. For the moment, anyway. Perhaps I'll feel differently about it in a few months. But just now, it's more important to me than anything,' she said frankly.

'Including me.' It was not a question.

'Haven't you put other things before me, Steve?' she said, gentle, but determined not to sacrifice something so dear to her on the altar of his selfishness.

For Patti realised now that Steve needed her more than she had ever needed him, after all. He was weak and he needed her strength. He was a taker and he needed her warm unstinting giving. He was surprisingly unsure and he needed her to bolster his confidence and self-esteem and assure him that he was all that he believed himself to be.

It seemed that Valerie had been unable or unwilling to supply those needs and so he had been unhappy and dissatisfied. Now he had turned back to Patti who had always provided love and loyalty and never criticised or condemned him. Patti did not regret that. But she did not know that she could be so unquestioning, so uncritical, so undemanding in the future. It seemed to her that there was a lot more to loving than Steve would ever know or realise.

Her thoughts sped to Ivor involuntarily. There was a man who would not be a disappointment to her if she loved him—if he loved her! Patti felt with a little wistfulness that it might be very wonderful to be loved by a man like Ivor. She wondered if the feelings she seemed to stir in him could ever lead to loving . . . She wondered why she could not stop thinking about Ivor Maynard!

Comparisons were odious. But she was not really comparing the two men, she assured herself. They were such totally different types that it was quite impossible. Besides, she did not know Ivor well enough to balance his good and bad points and decide that she liked him.

Patti smiled wryly at the thought that such a

cold-blooded assessment could have anything to do with liking. She did like Ivor and there was an end to it. However many faults he had must be outweighed by the charm and the warmth and the humour in him. She wished that Steve had not complicated matters by turning up just as she had been on the verge of believing that it might be possible to love twice in a lifetime . . .

Steve made no further attempt to dissuade her from going back and Patti knew he was disappointed, rather annoyed. But he was buoyant and she knew he would soon bob back, as confident and as cheerful as ever and quite unconvinced that she could really prefer nursing and sharing a flat with three other girls to being with him. No doubt he thought her pride was still smarting. Perhaps it was just as well that he did not know how doubtful her heart felt about the future he wanted her to spend with him . . .

They reached Hartlake in time for a drink in the Kingfisher before Jim Carver called "time". By chance, Joanne and John were in the pub. Patti introduced Steve as an old friend from home and sat back as he exercised his charm on her Hartlake friends, wondering why she did not experience the familiar thrill of pride in him.

He did have charm, of course. He was always much liked, easily accepted, very popular with everyone. She wondered why it had never occurred to her before that he was shallow, superficial, a born salesman who knew just how to sell himself as successfully as he sold the products of his firm.

She checked the disloyal criticism of him, wondering if his treatment of her still rankled so much that she could regard him with cool, critical eyes for the first time. It didn't change the way she felt about him, of course, she told herself firmly.

By chance, they sat in the same corner where she had so recently sat with Ivor. She realised with a shock of surprise that it was only two nights ago. It seemed that she had known him so much longer than that. They had slipped into a kind of intimacy without even realising it. It was really rather absurd to feel that she liked him so much and knew him so well when he was still almost a stranger.

She felt that odd, instinctive prickling at the roots of her hair which told her that eyes were boring into the back of her head. Patti turned, swiftly. She was not even surprised to meet Ivor's dark, unsmiling eyes.

She smiled slightly, rather too conscious of Steve's arm lying about her shoulders and Steve's personality dominating their small group and Steve's easy air of proprietary interest.

Almost immediately, Ivor looked away. He turned back to Jenefer Neal who stood with him at the bar counter, hand linked lightly in his arm and eager voice demanding his attention. Patti was near enough to catch some of the words and heard enough to learn that they had just returned from a show at the London Palladium.

She ought not to mind that he had speedily found a substitute companion for the evening. She ought not to mind the other woman's obvious satisfaction that she was with one of the most eligible bachelors at Hartlake. She ought not to mind the way he looked and smiled and spoke, or the sudden conviction that the staff nurse would console him in every way for any disappointment he might have felt because Patti had refused to spend the evening with him.

But she did mind . . . dreadfully.

She felt an acute stab of jealousy and a positive dislike of the staff nurse. She wanted to burst into tears. She wanted to rush into Ivor's arms and have him hold her, very close, very tight. She wanted to wipe out the hours she had spent with Steve and the evening he had obviously spent with Jenefer Neal as if they had never been.

She could not do any of those things. Patti turned her back on the couple and smiled with suspiciously sparkling brilliance at Steve and knew with a sick sense of dismay that she had foolishly tumbled into love with Ivor Maynard.

Whatever she had felt for Steve—and she had felt very deeply for a very long time—it did not compare with the wrenching upheaval of heart and mind and body and soul that had turned her world upside down.

Idiot girl, he had called her—and so she was, to love a man who was so heartfree and so untroubled by Steve's existence that he could look at Jenefer Neal in just that way and smile at her in just that way and put his arm about her to draw her against him in just that way . . . like a lover!

It was torment to see. But her gaze seemed drawn of its own volition and she unconsciously strained to hear what Ivor was saying as he bent his dark head to the staff nurse's receptive ear. Jenefer

Neal laughed and threw him a coquettishly reproachful glance—and then she smiled and nodded in a way that could only mean one thing.

Patti watched as they made their way through the press of people to the pub door, Ivor's arm about the girl's waist, and her hands were so tightly clenched that the nails dug fierce crescents into her soft palms . . .

Jenefer Neal was in a sunny frame of mind on the following day and that told its own story, Patti thought unhappily. The staff nurse positively oozed sweetness and light, and there was a hint of pitying condescension in the way she smiled at Patti when they passed each other in the corridor. Patti discovered the existence of very primitive instincts that she had not known she possessed.

'Cat got at the cream,' Marian Foster commented dryly, helping Patti to make beds and tidy lockers in readiness for rounds. She jerked her head in the direction of the staff nurse as she spoke. 'She's telling everyone who'll listen what a marvellous evening she spent with Ivor Maynard last night.' She sighed in reluctant admiration. 'I don't know where that man gets his energy—*or* the time to be as busy as he always seems to be in that direction. Casanova was a mere novice by comparison, I should think!'

Patti said nothing.

Marian looked at her curiously, wondering if the registrar was the cause of the obvious feud between staff nurse and first-year as the grapevine rumoured. It was astonishing how rapidly the tiniest piece of gossip could travel about the hospital and be enlarged upon with each telling. She was glad that she had never attracted Ivor Maynard's doubtful notice and thus risked her reputation or Matron's disapproval.

But Marian would have staked a tidy sum on Patti Parkin's level head and maturity and her ability to recognise a rake when she saw one and keep him at a safe distance. So she was rather inclined to discount much of the gossip about the first year's supposed relationship with the registrar.

Besides, it was all around Hartlake that the distinctive, red-haired junior nurse had been soundly kissed in the hospital garden by a man who had accompanied her to the Kingfisher much later in the day. Another juicy titbit for the gossips, Marian thought dryly.

'I don't suppose you're much interested in Neal's love life,' she said lightly as they moved on to the next bed. 'Or jealous! By all accounts, your taste runs to blond men.' Her eyes twinkled with mischief as Patti's expression betrayed her. 'I told you there's no such thing as a private life in this place, ducky,' she teased. 'Who is he?'

Patti smiled wryly. Then, suddenly, without rhyme or reason, she heard herself saying carelessly: 'You must mean Steve, my fiancé. He came here to meet me yesterday. I expect we were seen together.' It was an odd sort of pride that compelled the words, spoken loudly enough for Jenefer Neal to hear as she made her way down the ward. But she was suddenly very determined that neither the staff nurse nor anyone else should suppose that she had any reason to dislike or resent Ivor's involvement with another woman.

'I didn't know you were engaged!' Marian exclaimed, pleased for the cheerful and hard-working junior who was so popular with almost everyone.

'Proof that it *is* possible to have a private life even at Hartlake,' Patti returned, a little tart. It was too late to retract that impulsive statement and she wondered how long it would be before it reached Ivor's ears. She had no real reason to suppose that it would matter to him, she reminded herself bleakly. She was just a girl in his life that he had not managed to seduce—and that might be her only claim to remembrance as far as he was concerned . . .

CHAPTER TEN

MR Willis had been propped up on pillows to prevent the respiratory problems that so often followed the administering of anaesthetics. He did look better, Patti saw with relief. But he did not seem to know where he was and he mistook her for his dead wife when she was sent to wash him. She knew he was still shocked after surgery, and confused by pain-killing drugs, and her bright hair seemed to remind him very much of the Lil he had lost and still mourned.

No one was anxious about him. He was making good progress and Mr Manning's houseman spent only a few obligatory minutes beside his bed before hurrying on to the next patient.

There was no reason for Patti to be anxious, but she could not shake off that vague heaviness of heart whenever she did anything for him or passed by his bed as she went about her work.

It was not a very good morning. Somehow Sister Percival had discovered that Patti had returned to the ward in the guise of a visitor on the previous afternoon. She had not been very pleased, pointing out that his own family had not been allowed to visit Mr Willis so soon after his operation and that while she could appreciate Patti's concern and her attachment to the elderly patient, she did not approve of the manner in which her junior nurse had circumvented her orders.

'I believe you know why I sent you off the ward, Nurse,' she said quietly. 'I'm very disappointed that you were so underhand in sneaking on to the ward while my back was turned. You knew that I would have refused permission for you to visit Mr Willis and so you were very careful not to ask me for it.'

'Yes, Sister. I'm sorry, Sister.'

Ann Percival relented. The girl did not look at all happy. All her sparkle had fled for some unknown reason. She was subdued, heavy-eyed.

'No harm done, as it happens. I know that you were warned in PTS not to get emotionally involved with patients, but I don't know that I'm too rigid about that. Caring and concern and genuine compassion are emotions that every good nurse must feel towards the patients, I believe. You show a great deal of promise as a nurse, you know. Your work is extremely satisfactory. But you mustn't allow your heart to rule your head if you wish to remain at Hartlake.'

Patti could not be deaf to that veiled threat. Promising or not, her training would come to an abrupt end if she continued to disrupt the smooth running of the ward.

'No, Sister,' she said meekly.

'And do try to co-operate with Nurse Neal,' Ann Percival added. 'Her manner may be a little unfortunate at times, but she is a qualified nurse with a great deal of experience and you simply must not undermine her authority on the ward. Such behaviour can only lessen the respect that patients have always had for our profession.'

'Yes, Sister . . .' Feeling thoroughly chastened, although the ward sister had not once raised her voice or even addressed her with any particular sharpness of tone, Patti had escaped from the office.

She did not even have the doubtful comfort of seeing Ivor that morning. It was not one of Mr Manning's operating days and those patients who had undergone surgery on the previous day were all doing so well that they could be dealt with by his houseman. There was no need for Ivor to visit Currie Ward.

Patti wanted to see him if only to confirm that bolt from the blue of the night before. It would not help to be convinced that loving him was not just an absurd fancy, of course. She did not deceive herself that loving someone like Ivor was the highway to happiness. It was much more likely that he would make her very unhappy indeed.

By the time she went to lunch, the news that she was engaged had travelled along the grapevine and she cursed her impetuous tongue as friends came up to her, eager for details. It was impossible to deny it without admitting to an out and out lie—and she supposed that her engagement to Steve had been more or less renewed by her behaviour. She knew he was confident that she would marry him once he had secured a divorce—and it was rather too late to regret the lovemaking which had restored their relationship to its former intimacy.

Steve was still very dear. Old habits died hard and he had been an important part of her life for a long time. Perhaps she *would* marry him when he was free. Perhaps she could find a degree of contentment with him even if her feeling for him was not the all-embracing love she had supposed it to be until Ivor Maynard walked into her life.

There was no future in loving him. She had only to remember his reputation, the heartaches he had caused with his inability to maintain his interest in any woman for long. He did not promise much happiness for any girl who was fool enough to love him, Patti thought bleakly.

If she heeded Sister's advice and refused to allow her heart to rule her head, she would promptly forget all about Ivor and concentrate on her nursing career until she found it possible to think of Steve as the real love of her life all over again. It might be three years before he could get his divorce and she could use that time to good purpose at Hartlake . . .

On her way back to the ward, she saw Ivor in Main Hall. He was by the reception desk with some papers in his hand, talking earnestly and at length. His silver-haired companion was listening intently, nodding from time to time.

Heart thudding, mouth suddenly dry and stomach churning wildly, Patti paused by the big notice-board and pretended to read details of the forthcoming fête organised by the Friends of Hartlake Hospital.

She wondered if she dared to attract his attention. She felt sure that he had only to glance at her to know the tumult of her feelings. There was no need to question the way she felt about him, after all. Her heart had almost leaped out of her breast with eager delight at the sight of that tall figure in the conventional dark suit. No white coat, she registered automatically. Off duty—or just taking a brief break from the demands of his job as junior registrar to a very clever and distinguished consultant?

The discussion came to an end. Patti saw the two men shake hands out of the corner of her eye. Then he began to walk across Main Hall in her direction. She held her breath.

Ivor saw her, nodded . . . so casually that her heart sank like a stone. Such an absent, meaningless gesture of recognition that he might have bestowed on the slightest acquaintance! Such a brief smile, without warmth or interest! Such an indifferent glance from dark eyes that she had known to spark and glow with sudden, exciting fire!

Patti was no fool. She understood the meaning of that casual nod, that careless smile, that failure to stop and exchange even the merest word with her. She was dismissed. She was no longer of any interest. She must not suppose that they were friends just because he had kissed her a few times in a way that meant nothing to his kind.

Jenefer Neal's charms must have been very potent, she thought heavily. Well, didn't she know what he was? Wasn't he the casual, uncaring lover of any girl who briefly took his fancy and could be persuaded into bed? And if he didn't get what he wanted at the first or second or even third time of trying, wasn't it obvious that he would simply look round for someone who did not disappoint him? Had she really thought that she might be something special in his life? She was as green as any of the juniors who had fallen such easy prey to his sensuality!

She was swamped with utter despair, an ache of misery such as she had never known even in the early days of losing Steve. She had thought she knew all about the pain of loving. How wrong could a girl be?

That evening, she settled down with her books to study, but she was soon interrupted by a telephone call from Steve. She wanted to cut him short but she checked the impulse and did her best to answer him like the Patience of old who had loved him and tried to be everything he wanted. But she was Patti these days and it was difficult to go back to thinking and feeling like Patience, she thought wryly. Patti was hopelessly in love with another man and there was no comfort in Steve's affection, Steve's need, Steve's irritation that she was no longer free to be with him at the drop of a hat.

She went back to her books. But her mood had been destroyed. She had never felt less like studying.

Jacqui was out for the evening. Phyllida was smocking a tiny dress for her sister's baby. She was clever with her fingers and Patti watched for a few minutes, admiring and envying the skill. Kate had decided to wash and set her blonde hair.

Patti was grateful that the initial excitement of her supposed engagement had died down. The three girls had bombarded her with questions and exclamations and affectionate reproaches, obviously genuine in their delight for her and very young in their belief that she could not want for anything more in life if she had found a man to marry her. So much for Women's Lib, Patti had thought, wryly amused despite her heartache.

Very much on edge, she had come close to denying the whole thing—and then asked herself if it mattered. As far as Hartlake in general and Ivor Maynard in particular were concerned, it might be as well if she was believed to be engaged to Steve. It would provide her with an excellent reason to refuse invitations from other men. It would convince Ivor that she was not interested in him or affected by his relationship with Jenefer Neal or anyone else—and that was particularly important. She loved him, but there was no need for him to know it, she thought proudly. She did not think she could bear it if he knew that he had captured her heart without even really trying!

It was a beautiful evening and Patti felt stifled by the confines of the flat. She decided to go for a walk. The dingy streets that surrounded the hospital were not very inviting. Patti did not even notice. She did not realise that she was in Clifton Street until she saw the unmistakable figure of Ivor Maynard striding along the pavement towards her . . . or, rather, towards his flat, she thought, suddenly aware where her feet had led her by chance.

It would be too pointed to turn and hurry back the way she had come. She must seem as casual, as unconcerned, as indifferent as he was, she told herself resolutely. She would pretend that she was on her way to call on Joanne. She glanced at the house numbers as she walked on. She had to pass the tall house that contained his flat, but she was pretty sure that he would reach the steps and run up them and let himself in before she reached him.

Ivor paused, waited. He had not meant to pass her without a word earlier in the day, but he had been late for an appointment, delayed by a chance meeting with the Dean of the Medical School, preoccupied with a variety of problems. Even so, he would have spoken if there had been the smallest encouragement in her manner. She had glanced at him coolly, reducing him to the status of stranger. He had been struck by her failure to smile. It had seemed to him like an unmistakable brush-off.

She had seen him with Jenefer Neal in the Kingfisher. If she had heard that the staff nurse had spent the night with him, as was likely with the damnably efficient hospital grapevine and Jenefer's equally damnable readiness to advertise their relationship, then Patti had probably decided that she wanted nothing more to do with him. Now, Ivor wanted very much to talk to her, to explain that the way in which she had entered the pub last night, holding hands with the man who had come back into her life and glowing with the warmth and excitement that came from lovemaking, had driven him into Jenefer's willing arms on a surge of jealous anger and dismay.

He wanted to find out if Patti really cared for her former fiancé, or if she was just clinging to the sentimental belief that she was still in love with him. He wanted to know if there was any hope at all if he allowed himself to love her. He wanted to tell her that she meant more to him than any woman he had ever known and that there had been no pleasure, no delight and very little satisfaction in making love to Jenefer. He wanted very much to hold Patti to his heart and know the warm and eager and utterly generous response that was only one of the reasons why she was so special, so unexpectedly dear.

As she reached him, he smiled.

Patti's heart bounded. 'Ivor . . .' she said uncertainly, forced to stop because he blocked her path, hoping eyes and voice and that absurd tendency to colour up would not betray her delight that he had waited to speak to her. Perhaps he did like her, she thought wistfully. Perhaps he was offering her his friendship—cold comfort but better than nothing.

'Patti . . .' he said, mocking her gently, dark eyes warm with teasing.

'I'm on my way to see Jo,' she said quickly, so that he should not suppose she was haunting his doorstep in the hope of seeing him.

'She's expecting you?'

Patti hesitated. She found she could not tell an outright lie. 'No.'

He took his keys from his pocket. 'Come in for a drink,' he said with a casual, light friendliness that was intended to put her at her ease. 'I've something to tell you.'

She looked at him doubtfully. 'What is it?'

'Over a drink,' he said firmly, mounting the steps and inserting his key in the lock.

Patti discovered that she had no option but to follow him into the high-ceilinged hall. 'Is it important?'

He looked down at her with a rueful gleam in his dark eyes. Her reluctance to be alone with him was painfully obvious. 'Don't trust me at all, do you, girl? I'm not luring you into my den of iniquity in order to seduce you,' he said lightly.

Then the colour did leap, flaming in her small face. So did the involuntary retort. 'You've no need of me with all the Jenefer Neals there are in the world,' she said, equally light but tart.

He laughed. 'You're well informed.' He opened the door of his flat, ushered her through to the attractive and comfortable sitting-room.

'Your affairs make headlines.'

'You mustn't believe everything you hear about me, Patti.'

'I'm not particularly interested in what you do,' she said coolly, and that lie came without any hesitation. 'Your exploits begin to be boring, anyway. I seem to have heard the same stories about you with different girls ever since I came to Hartlake.'

She saw from the flicker of his eyes and a little tightening of his mouth that the words had hit home. But he merely smiled and crossed to pour the drinks.

'Sit down,' he said hospitably.

Patti did not want to sit down or accept a drink. She wanted to rush away to the safety of her flat and her friends so that she would not be tempted to atone for the harshness of her words by putting her arms about him. She wondered why she should suppose that anything she said or did could hurt him.

She perched on the arm of the sofa to indicate that she did not mean to stay. 'What did you want to tell me, Ivor?'

He glanced at her, slightly rueful. 'It isn't good. Your Mr Willis died this evening . . . cardiac arrest. It was very sudden, quite unexpected. I've just come from the ward.'

'Oh, no!' She was dismayed. Her eyes abruptly filled with tears. It seemed the final blow in a wretched day. 'He seemed to be doing so well, too!'

'Yes. I'm sorry.' He wanted to catch her into his arms and kiss away the tears that shone in those bright eyes, threatening to spill.

She shook her head, tried to smile at him, needlessly ashamed of her emotional reaction to the news. 'Silly of me . . . I knew it was going to happen. He had no heart to go on. He missed his wife too much and he couldn't face the future without her. He talked about her so much. He said . . .' She broke off, bit her lip, went on again: '. . . that her hair was my colour when they were married. I suppose that's why he took such a fancy to me.'

'Red hair has always been a weakness with me, too,' Ivor said, his light touch lifting the moment. He put his hand to her bright curls, twined his fingers in them, so soft and silky and clinging. 'I've taken a fancy to you, myself.' His voice softened, deepened on the words.

'You and your fancies . . .' Patti tried to remember how meaningless it all was to him, but her heart was beating like a wild thing in her throat. The light, mocking, would-be amused words died away as he bent over her with intent, kissed her. It was only a game to him, she knew, a meaningless, exciting titillation of the senses that seemed as necessary to him as breathing. But it was heaven to her to know the warm pressure of his mouth on her own, soft but seeking. She did not mean to respond. She simply could not help it.

Ivor put his hand to her slender throat, arched for his kiss. He stroked the soft skin, caressing. She quivered. He ran his fingers lightly down her throat to the soft, sensitive mound of her breast, covered by the thin stuff of her print frock. She quickened at his touch, caught her breath. His kiss became fractionally more demanding. She resisted momentarily. Then she sighed against his lips and her arm stole about his neck and her body relaxed against him, soft and yielding.

'Patti . . . ?' he said, urgent.

She recognised his need, as fierce as her own. He wanted her—and she did not much care in that moment that it was only a fleeting sexual desire that prompted him. She recalled the way she had given herself to Steve in cold blood. That was a great deal worse than giving herself to mutual and ecstatic wanting, she felt. Loving was giving, after all—and she loved this man with all of her, heart and soul and body, in a way that she had never felt for Steve for all the years of caring.

'Yes,' she said, quick and warm. 'Oh, *yes* . . . !'

At those eager words, Ivor drew her up and into his arms, kissed her again. He was fired with a warm tenderness as well as the eager passion of a sensual nature. He wanted her so much. He knew that he loved her. Their coming together would not be just another sexual encounter for him but a turning point, a total commitment to one woman for the first and last time in his life.

He lifted her into his arms and carried her through to the bedroom. As he laid her on the wide bed, she smiled and held out her arms to him in a gesture of giving that caught at his heart.

Ivor undressed her slowly, with tender hands and lingering kisses to allay her doubts and fears. He drew in his breath sharply at her nude loveliness, paying homage with his eyes, the almost reverent touch of his hand, the burying of his lips in her soft breast.

With a little gasp, Patti drew him down to her on a tidal wave of wanting that engulfed them both and soon her slight body was shuddering with the flooding delight that she had begun to despair of ever knowing in any man's embrace.

He was the kind of lover that every woman dreams about, sensual but tender, caring and considerate, ensuring the wonder and the magic and then the ultimate ecstasy with his expertise and intuitive understanding of her needs.

They lay in close embrace for a long time, without words, content. Patti did not want to think or feel beyond these precious moments of being with him, held by him, holding him close.

She loved the length of his lean, hard body against her own. She loved the dark head resting on the pillow and she impulsively touched her lips to the thick black curls. She loved the little smile that leaped instantly to his dark eyes, crinkling them at the corners. Her heart swelled and she laid her hand along the lean cheek, moved to kiss the smiling, sensual mouth.

His arms tightened abruptly. 'There's lovely you

are, girl,' he murmured softly, the Welsh suddenly very liquid in the deep, drawling voice. 'Born to give, you are, *cariad* . . .'

'*Cariad*,' she echoed, liking the lilt of the word and the warm way he used it. She smiled at him, curious. 'What is it?'

'A Welsh term of endearment. It means dearest, darling—whatever the heart wants it to mean.' He raised himself on to his elbow, smiling into her shining eyes. 'I haven't said it to a girl since I was thirteen. Come to think of it, she had red hair, too. Gwyneth, she was—prettiest girl in the class.'

'The first of your many conquests, I suppose. And I'm not likely to be the last!' She had meant to be light, teasing, for she must not seem to reproach him when she had so little right. But the words came out sharp, accusing, shattering the precious intimacy and the delicate understanding. She had suddenly seen a square of black chiffon across a chair.

Black and spangled with sequins, she had last seen it about Jenefer Neal's neck as she stood with Ivor in the Kingfisher. It was a timely and very painful reminder that all her loving, all her giving, all her wealth of wanting could not alter the fact that he was an incorrigible and untrustworthy rake.

Last night, the staff nurse had lain in this bed, in his arms, she thought bleakly. Tonight, she had been his delight. She could not help wondering who would be the next girl to know the kiss, the caress, the urgent and exciting embrace of this highly-sexed and sensual man.

He had taken her without one word of love.

Warmth, tenderness, sensual and sensitive urging, certainly. *Patti*, he had said, urgent. *There's lovely you are*, he had said, lilting. *Cariad*, he had said, meaning anything or nothing. But not *I love you*. Not one word of love, of real and lasting need, of promise for the future.

What future was there for any girl who loved him but heartache and humiliation and hopeless longing . . . ?

CHAPTER ELEVEN

IVOR stiffened at the words. But he thought he understood. Like all women, she wanted to own him, body and soul, and she was jealous of the girls he had known and lightly loved in the past. For the first time, he understood and entered into those kind of feelings. He wanted Patti to be his, completely and for ever. He did not want to think about the men she might have loved, the man to whom she had once been engaged. The past was behind them and could be forgotten. The future belonged to them both.

'I know how it seems,' he said quietly. 'There have been a lot of girls. No point in denying what the whole world knows, is it? No one like you, Patti . . .'

He leaned to kiss her. She pushed him away. 'Every girl is different. That's the attraction, isn't it? You'd be very bored if you had to settle for one woman!'

'Not if you were the woman.' He began to trace the curves of her lovely breast with his long fingers, slow and lingering, his dark eyes warm with remembered and reminding delight. 'Do you think I don't mean it? I do, Patti.'

She trembled at the look in his eyes, at that tentative, teasing, titillating touch. She wished she could believe him, but she could only think of the careless way he had walked from the Kingfisher with his arm about Jenefer Neal and the light way he had taken the other woman to his bed. His claim to want only her was not very convincing, she thought heavily.

Just now, he would say anything to persuade her back into his arms. Just now, he was ready to make love again. She knew that she would be lost if she allowed him to draw her close. The magic was already weaving its subtle spell about her senses. She kissed him, quick, hard. Then she sat up and reached for her scattered clothes. 'No more, Ivor . . .'

He put an arm over her. '*Cariad*, don't go away,' he said softly, persuasively. 'The night is ours . . .'

Patti resisted the poetry in the words, the tone, the soft sigh of the endearment. She slipped from the bed and began to dress while he watched her.

Dressed, she moved towards the door. 'I'll make coffee,' she said, as though it was the most natural thing in the world that she should be so much at home in his flat and so much at ease with him. It was, to Patti. She felt that they had known each other for ever, that they belonged together, two halves of a whole, and so it hurt all the more that he would probably never feel that way about her. She did not dare to deceive herself, to dream that there could be no end to this golden idyll. She was a very temporary need in his life, like all the others . . .

Ivor joined her in the kitchen, running his hands through his rumpled hair. The fragrant smell of the coffee pervaded the room and Patti was at the sink, rinsing the glasses they had used earlier.

She looked so pretty and so appealing in her Hartlake uniform frock, the faint glow of their lovemaking still lingering in her cheeks and in her bright eyes, that his heart contracted on a sudden surge of loving.

He went to stand behind her, put his arms about her and touched his lips to that richly beautiful hair. There was so much he wanted to say and such a fear in him of not being believed.

Words were too easy. He must find a number of ways to prove that he loved her, without words. It might take some considerable time and effort to live down the reputation which could not encourage her to take him seriously, he thought wryly.

Patti relaxed against him briefly and smiled up at him. She wished with all her heart that she could believe the warmth and the tenderness in his dark eyes. But it was only the mood of the moment. Tomorrow, it would be forgotten. Tomorrow, he would be looking at another girl as though he loved her. Ivor had a gift for making a woman feel that she was the only one in the world for him. That was the particular danger of his charm. The sorrow of it was that too many girls had believed it to be true.

Patti, older and wiser, did not dare to dream that he could really mean the way he looked, the way he held her, the way he said her name.

For that brief hour he had been a lover and she had no regrets. Except that they might have been friends and now that could never be. Friends could turn into lasting lovers. But lovers could never go back to being friends.

'Will you come away with me?' he asked, a little

brusque because it mattered so much. 'You must be due for some days off and I can arrange leave. God knows I've earned it!' He turned her in his arms, smiled into her eyes. 'We need to get away from the gossips and find out more about each other, Patti. Kissing in cupboards and snatching an occasional hour in bed isn't very satisfactory, is it? It's served well enough in the past, but you deserve better than that, girl. My people have a cottage on the Norfolk coast that we've always used for weekends and holidays. It will be ideal for our purpose . . .'

He was persuasive and Patti was terribly tempted, but she knew it would be disastrous to go away with him. There would be too much to remember and too much to mourn when another girl took her place in his life. She knew it had to happen. Leopards didn't lose their spots. Rakes didn't reform.

For the moment, he wanted her, and that made it a wonderful world. But it would not last. He was not the type to love in earnest, to give up his freedom, to be content with one woman for the rest of his life. She would be all kinds of a fool if she allowed herself to believe that she was the one girl out of all that he had known to bring about a change of heart in this man.

For the sake of her heart and her pride and her peace of mind, she had to be the one to make the break—here and now before she fell even deeper into loving him. There were depths to Ivor that she had never suspected and she knew that he could become too dear, too important, too necessary to her happiness.

'There won't be any more kissing in cupboards or going to bed, Ivor,' she said lightly but firmly, moving out of his embrace. 'Tonight shouldn't have happened.' She smiled wryly. 'You're too much temptation,' she went on, using his own words against him with a levity that did her credit when her heart was protesting so violently at her level head's decision. 'But it doesn't have to mean anything, you know—and it doesn't have to lead to a full-scale affair.'

Ivor frowned. He did not understand—and he did not want to believe what her words so obviously implied.

'You're the only girl I've ever known to think so,' he said carefully, his heart thudding with the fear that she meant to slam shut the door that had opened to give him a glimpse of what life could be with her to share it.

'Oh, Ivor! Not every girl has to fall head over heels in love with you, surely!' she mocked in gentle reproach. 'Do you suppose that a girl can't enjoy sex for its own sake with a very attractive man? That's an old-fashioned point of view!'

His eyes darkened. 'Then I suppose I am old-fashioned,' he said quietly.

'I'm sorry if I've shattered an illusion, but I'm not the least bit in love with you,' Patti declared brightly, lying with the desperate need to be believed. 'You obviously haven't heard that I'm going to marry Steve, after all. The grapevine isn't as efficient as I've been led to believe!'

Ivor felt as though he had been punched very hard in the solar plexus. He wondered if he could cope with the twin shocks of loving her and losing her in one fell swoop. He had no experience to draw on, he thought wryly. All those women in his life and not one had caused him a moment's real heartache, a moment's real regret for the might-have-been. Deeply and irrevocably in love at last, he knew that losing Patti would mean a lifetime of both.

'You're happy about that, I suppose,' he said slowly. He loved her but he did not know her well enough to read the truth in her lovely eyes, her pretty voice. He had thought there was all the truth a man could want in the way she had kissed him, held him, clung to him.

'Well, of course! I can't remember a time when I didn't want to marry Steve!'

And that was true as far as it went. No need to tell him that she seemed to have outgrown the youthful giving of a heart that had not known the half of what it meant to love until she met him.

She did not want to know that he loved her, Ivor thought heavily. There was no point in trying to tell her, trying to prove it to her. She felt nothing for him but the kind of attraction that he had known for too many girls. The biter bit, he realised ruefully.

Perhaps he had been heading for this come-uppance for a very long time. Perhaps it was a sad thing that all those girls he had taken and discarded so lightly could not know the way he was feeling at this moment. He had not realised the cruelty of using them for his sensual satisfaction while he waited for the one girl who could really matter to him to come along. It was ironic, but perhaps it was poetic justice that having found her, she should not want him!

'Then I'm happy for you, Patti,' he said warmly and discovered, to his surprise, that he meant the words.

Her happiness *was* all-important. He must not suppose that it lay with him after only a few days of knowing each other. It would be an appalling conceit to believe that he was the only man who could make and keep her happy for ever.

Patti managed to smile. 'That's nice of you . . .'

He was so much nicer than she had known, she thought, warming to the sincerity in his tone. That made it all the harder to break with him. She fought the impulse to hurl herself into his arms and confess that she had lied.

Ivor walked her to the door of the Nurses' Home, assuring her that he needed to look in on a patient on Paterson when she protested that it was not necessary for him to accompany her.

There, in the shadows, he took her into his arms and kissed her for the last time, very gently.

It took all Patti's strength of mind to accept that kiss with cool lips, only just responding to the warm pressure of his mouth.

'The way you feel about me doesn't matter,' Ivor said quietly, holding her for a moment longer, his dark head pressed hard against her cheek. 'I just want you to know that you were special, Patti . . .' Then he was gone.

It was her own doing. She could have known a great deal of happiness with him until he tired, as he inevitably would. But it would have meant an agony of heartbreak in the end. Losing Steve had hurt but she had survived. Losing Ivor once he became a vital need in her life would be too much for any heart to bear.

Patti knew that she had done the right thing, the only thing. But something within her that had quickened to a new and lovely dream died a very painful death as she watched his tall figure striding into the night.

She could not cry for that lost dream. Some things went too deep for tears . . .

There was a new patient in the bed that Mr Willis had occupied when Patti went into the ward the next morning. She could not grieve for the little man who had not wanted to get over the loss of his leg, but she thought very kindly of him. In a way, he had brought her and Ivor together. She would never forget him any more than she would ever forget Ivor.

The new patient was the young motor-cyclist that Ivor had talked about, transferred to Currie from the Intensive Care Unit. With all the buoyant resilience of youth, his body was making a good recovery from the crash that had killed his girl-friend, but a feeling of guilt was obviously weighing very heavily on his mind and spirits.

He talked about the accident to anyone who would listen, almost obsessively remembering and recounting every detail. He talked at length to Patti about the fifteen-year-old Maureen, for she was a sympathetic and understanding listener who made the time to let him talk it out of his system.

She comforted him as best as she could, knowing that he did not want to be told that at eighteen he would soon get over his feeling for the dead girl and find someone else, that time would heal the loss and erase the sense of guilt. Just now, he wanted and needed to believe that he would love her for ever. It was his memorial to the girl who had died because he had recklessly taken a corner at speed on a wet night.

They were even busier than usual on the ward that week and the time that Patti spent with the injured boy in Bed 3 meant that the other first year was doing more than her fair share of the ward chores. Madeleine Long was too good-natured to grumble. Sister Percival saw that it was doing the boy a great deal of good to pour out his grief and remorse to the warm-hearted junior who allowed him to take up so much of her time. She had a quiet word with Jenefer Neal who refrained from scolding Patti for dawdling, for spending too much time with one patient, for allowing her work to be neglected while she lingered at his bedside.

Patti noticed that the staff nurse had ceased to harass her and even smiled at her now and again. She wondered with a heavy heart if Ivor's renewed attentions were responsible for the softening of the other girl's attitude. She could understand the dislike and resentment that the senior nurse had felt towards her when Ivor was making little secret of his interest. Now, she felt sick with dismay whenever she saw them together on or off the ward, talking and laughing and obviously on very friendly terms—and it did not help that their relationship seemed to be common knowledge among her fellow-nurses.

She tried very hard not to think about Ivor and she was glad of Michael Keen's presence on the ward to give her an alternative object for her thoughts and feelings. She needed to help and comfort him just as much as he needed her warm interest and concern. Caring about him and his unhappiness helped her to cope with her own. Devoting herself to him as much as possible meant that she did not have time during the day for futile longing however wakeful and restless and unhappy the nights might be for her.

It was impossible not to encounter Ivor on the ward and in the hospital precincts. But she could fall back on the etiquette that maintained a wide gulf between registrar and first-year nurse—and he was so casual, so cool, so almost impersonal that they might never have shared those glorious moments of unforgettable intimacy.

Patti supposed it was easy for him to dismiss her as he had dismissed all the others. It would be very foolish to believe that she *had* been "special" where a man like Ivor was concerned. If she was different from all the other girls he had known, it could only be because she had ended the affair and not clung to him desperately long after he had lost interest, she decided.

She could not have meant much to him or he would not have accepted her claim to be engaged to Steve without some protest. Perhaps Ivor despised her for falling so readily into his arms and into his bed when she was supposed to be in love with another man and planning to marry him. Patti admitted fairly that she would have little liking or respect for herself if it had been true.

It hurt that she had probably lost his good opinion with that proud pretence. But it would hurt less in the long run that she had forced herself to end an association that could not lead to anything but heartache and a lasting disappointment. Ivor had liked her, but he had never come near to loving her. That was just another dream that had crumbled into dust.

Steve was monopolising her leisure hours as much as possible and Patti, too unhappy to care very much how she spent that free time, fell in with his wishes and plans just as she had in the past. But so far she had managed to avoid a repeat of the lovemaking for which she had no heart at all. To lie in Steve's arms in cold blood when she had such wonderful memories of Ivor's sensual and sensitive embrace was not to be endured.

Patti knew that she must soon tell Steve that she no longer loved him and would never marry him. But while he was around, telephoning her, taking her out and meeting her friends, there was no reason for anyone to suspect that her engagement was sheer fabrication. She needed the prop of that little deception during those first difficult days when she was so tempted to weaken and run after Ivor as fast as she could.

She knew it was wrong to use Steve to her own ends. Letters from home told her that he and Valerie had parted and that her cousin was desperately unhappy. Her mother wrote that Steve was working in London and wondered if Patti had seen anything of him. The letter was so carefully and tactfully phrased that she knew, dismayed and a little angry, that Valerie had told the world just why Steve had left her after only a few months of marriage. It was not Valerie's fault. Steve had been much too sure that she still loved him and would forgive and forget just for the asking!

Patti could not help feeling that he had forfeited all right to her love and loyalty when he broke their engagement and married Valerie with so little regard for the years that they had shared as lovers. She doubted if she could have welcomed him back with a truly glad heart even if she had not fallen in love with Ivor. She hoped with all her heart that Steve would go back to his wife if she could convince him that there was no future in caring for her, after all. But it had always been the hardest thing in the world to make him accept that he could not have everything he wanted in life, she thought wryly.

Although he must sense from her coolness and her reluctance and her general behaviour that she did not mean to resume their relationship just as though nothing had happened to interrupt it, he still seemed confident that she would eventually agree to give up nursing and live with him until they could be married.

Patti knew it would never happen, although at one time she had wondered if the long and steadfast devotion to Steve was more reliable than the fierce flame of loving.

She had known Steve so well and so long. She

had scarcely known Ivor at all. But the heart seemed to have its own reasons for loving and she knew in the depth of her being that Ivor was the one man she would love and want for the rest of her life. She could not settle for second best with Steve . . .

He took her to a hospital dance one evening. Such functions were always well attended and led to a number of flirtations and sometimes lasting affairs between members of the staff. Patti and Steve were with a cheerful and rather noisy group that included Joanne and John, Daisy and her fiancé Gavin Fletcher among others. Three tables had been pushed together so that they were one large party at the edge of the dance floor.

A seemingly casual question had elicited the information from Jo that Ivor was not likely to be present that evening. So Patti felt she could relax and she was just beginning to enjoy herself when that strange sixth sense told her of his gaze. She wondered if it was the white frock or her unmistakable hair that had caught his eye as he glanced across the crowded dance floor.

He was with Jenefer Neal. Of course, she thought numbly. The staff nurse still held his interest and they had been on very friendly terms for much longer than was apparently usual for Ivor. She was sparkling and animated, quite lovely in a vivid flame-coloured frock that suited her dark hair and creamy complexion, and she was obviously eager to draw everyone's attention to the fact that Ivor was her escort. She stood by his side, tall and elegant and rather striking, very confident.

Patti's heart shook as their eyes met. She did not

know that the smile fled from her eyes almost instantly because she saw Jenefer Neal on his arm, clinging and confident. She only saw that Ivor looked away with casual unconcern, spoke to the girl at his side and swept her on to the dance floor.

It was crowded and Patti caught only the occasional glimpse of them as they danced. But it was enough to tear her heart to shreds. For he held the staff nurse very close, dark heads together like lovers, and there was the warmth of affection in the dark eyes that would not meet Patti's although they came near from time to time as they danced with their respective partners.

Twice, she stumbled over Steve's feet because she was welling with misery. The first time, he smiled and said nothing. The second time, he suggested that they should sit down, a little impatient with her clumsiness.

'I'm sorry,' she said penitently. 'I'm out of practice.'

'Tired, more likely. I wish you'd give up this damn job, Patience!' He guided her through the press of people to their table.

Patti's eyes sparked with annoyance but she said nothing. It was not the time or the place and she did not have the heart to go on with an argument that was rapidly becoming a bore.

CHAPTER TWELVE

It seemed that they would never agree on something that was very important to her. To Steve, nursing was just a job that anyone could do. To Patti, it was a rewarding and fulfilling way of life for all its demands on her energies and emotions and she was grateful that Hartlake, with its famous and sacred traditions, had recognised that she had the necessary qualities to be a good and caring nurse.

Sometimes she wondered how much longer she could continue to feel any liking for Steve. She would always know a lingering fondness for him because of golden days when they had been young and in love. But that was sheer sentiment and it did not deter her from realising that she did not like him very much these days. It was a little sad to realise that she might have gone on loving him a little for the rest of her life if he had not come in pursuit of her and given her both opportunity and reason to compare him with Ivor.

To her dismay, Ivor and Jenefer Neal came to join their party at the invitation of Gavin Fletcher. It was not in Steve's nature to show jealousy, even if he felt it, but Patti did not want to run the risk of betraying the effect that Ivor could have on her even if he virtually ignored her, which, at first, it seemed that he would do.

They exchanged brief and very casual greetings

as he and Jenefer sat down in a couple of vacant seats at their end of the grouped tables. The staff nurse was prepared to be friendly, smiling at Patti, admiring her frock and asking if she was enjoying the evening. She glanced at Steve with such pointed interest that Patti had no choice but to make the necessary introductions. She was thankful that Jenefer did not immediately demand to know if he was the fiancé that everyone was talking about. Rather constrained, she had merely described him as a friend, just as she usually did.

Steve was always at his ease in any gathering, winning friends and influencing people with his easy charm and confidence that made him such a successful salesman. Once, Patti had loved him for it. Now, she found that it irritated her. Once, it had been a natural and very attractive charm. Through the years, it had become too practised, too superficial and too conscious that he needed to sell himself as well as his famous company's products. It seemed to the sharply critical Patti that he could never forget that he was used to dealing with valuable and wealthy clients.

He chatted easily to Ivor and Jenefer while Patti sat and watched the dancing couples, taking no part in the conversation, careful not to look at Ivor, careful not to turn her head each time she heard his deep voice.

Steve seemed relaxed and at ease, but she knew that he did not like Ivor. He knew nothing about the registrar and certainly did not know of Patti's brief involvement with him. The dislike and the faint hostility that she sensed because she knew him so well could only stem from an awareness of certain qualities in another man that he lacked and which made him feel uncomfortably and rarely inferior.

But he did like Jenefer. It was obvious that she made him feel very much a man with her uncritical interest and admiration. Very soon, he asked her to dance and Patti observed dryly that the attractive staff nurse did not fall over his feet. Their steps matched perfectly.

Patti knew that Ivor was watching her rather than the dancing couples who swirled about the floor to the music. She would not turn to meet his eyes but she felt that odd, tingling excitement running through her veins. Then he put his hand on her shoulder in light but warm contact and she knew that she trembled at his touch. She thought ruefully that he probably knew it, too.

'Patti . . .'

She looked at him with a slightly tremulous smile. The unexpected warmth in his voice almost broke through her vulnerable defences.

'It's too long since I held you,' he said softly. 'May I have the pleasure . . . ?' There was just the hint of dancing mischief in those dark eyes as he murmured the conventional words with a great deal of unconventional meaning in his pleasant drawl.

Patti hesitated, heart and blood stirring in the swift, familiar response to him. Then she nodded and rose to her feet. Knowing it was madness, she went into his waiting arms.

Ivor held her at a slight distance, knowing that his body must betray the desire that consumed him. He had missed her terribly, ached for her constantly and found it damnably difficult to concentrate on the work that took him too often to Currie Ward. Patti was an enchantment such as he had never known. She was his dear delight, his lasting love— and she was in love with another man.

Ivor had always been a sensual man but there seemed to be no comfort or consolation for him in the company or the arms of other women. Jenefer had made a dead set for him. It had been too much of an effort to snub her and he had a sneaking sympathy for her feelings if they were anything like his own for Patti. So he had been pleasant to her when they met and he had taken her for the odd drink, the occasional meal. It had pleased her and eased his loneliness to some extent and he did not care very much what the gossips thought or said. His affairs had been talked about ever since his medical student days at Hartlake. It did not seem to matter if it was rumoured that this one was more serious than most.

He had decided to take his leave and go away for a few days. Work and other distractions were failing to lighten his spirits in any way. It was too poignant and too painful to see Patti at almost every turn. However it happened, she seemed to be everywhere that he went—on the ward, in the corridors, visiting various departments of the hospital, walking along the street in front of him, in the pub or in the company of mutual friends. He seemed to catch glimpses of that bright hair and lovely face and slender figure all the time, although it seemed unlikely that it could always be Patti.

Ivor wondered if every girl in the world was beginning to look like her!

He supposed that her thoughts and dreams and hopes for the future were revolving happily about the man she meant to marry and so it was not unexpected that she hurried away at his approach or pretended to be too busy to notice him on the ward or escaped as quickly as she could if she had to talk to him. He felt that she did not want to be reminded of the hour she had spent in his arms, warm and eager and sharing the delight and the ecstasy—and that was understandable in view of the engagement to another man that it seemed everyone at Hartlake but himself had known about.

Now, holding her, he knew that something undeniably sparked between them and it seemed that Patti believed it to be wiser and safer to keep him out of her life as much as she could. She had avoided him, scarcely smiled or spoke when they did run into each other on or off the ward, and had been very intent on emphasising her involvement with the fair-haired, smooth-talking and probably unreliable Steve Rawlings.

A doctor in a busy teaching hospital came into contact with a great many and varied types of people and learned to be a reasonably good judge of character. Patti's fiancé was a fairly predictable type, Ivor felt—and he marvelled that someone as perceptive and as sensitive as Patti could care so much for the man. But it might be that he was just too jealous to recognise his good qualities, he admitted wryly.

He smiled down at her and said softly: 'There's

pretty you are, all in white. Rehearsing, is it?'

She met the laughing eyes, looked away with a little colour rising in her small face. She had learned that he was very Welsh when he was teasing her in that gentle, endearing fashion. Her heart stirred. 'I don't know what you mean,' she said defensively.

'For the wedding, girl.'

'Oh . . .' Patti stumbled, almost tripped. There had seemed to be a touch of mockery in the light words and she panicked slightly. Had he found out that she was not really engaged to Steve? He would know that she had lied—and possibly why she had lied! Her pride shrank from the thought that her love for him might be dragged, protesting, into the light of day. He was quite capable of it, she suspected ruefully.

Ivor's arms tightened swiftly, almost protectively. 'All right . . . ?'

'Yes. Sorry, Ivor. I'm afraid I don't dance very well.'

He smiled into her eyes. 'As far as I'm concerned, you do everything well, Patti,' he said with unmistakable meaning.

She smiled uncertainly.

Ivor drew her close, so close that she thought he must feel the heavy thud of her heart, much too fast for the nearness of him. Then she realised the controlled but insistent throb of passion in that lean, taut body and knew that his hold was threatening to become an embrace. Her own senses tumbled and she was suddenly breathless. She did not dare to lean against him, to slide her arm up and about his neck as she longed to do. She was afraid that he would not hesitate to kiss her before all those watching eyes—and she knew she would kiss him back.

'This was a mistake,' he said abruptly, very tense. 'I want you too much.' His dark head was against her own. She felt the sigh of his breath against her cheek.

'I know the feeling,' she said with wry honesty. Her body was clamouring for him. Her heart was sad that the wanting in him owed nothing at all to love. 'I didn't want to dance with you, Ivor,' she told him, with reproach.

His eyes were warm. 'Yes, you did, *cariad*.'

Her heart quickened at the endearment she had never expected to hear again. Her hand tightened on his broad shoulder and her body came near to melting against him. They were entirely alone in that crowded and music-filled ballroom, oblivious to everything but each other. His lips were warm and gentle on her neck, tracing a route to her mouth with slow, insidious intent.

Then, suddenly, Patti was shaken by a vision of Jenefer or Felicity or any of his many women lying in his arms and hearing that soft, enchanting word on his lips and knowing the warm urgency of desire in his embrace. It was very tempting to believe that his feeling for her went beyond mere physical wanting, but he had never given her any reason to think so, she reminded herself heavily. Love was a word he did not use.

She gave his shoulder a little, angry shake and jerked her head away from the touch of his lips. 'I wish you'd get out of my life!' she said, almost passionately, almost meaning it. She was frightened by the intensity of her feeling for him and she knew that she would do anything he asked, go to the ends of the earth with him if he should wish it. It was even more frightening to the heart that loved him that he would obviously never ask anything of her but a brief, sensual interlude of physical delight.

'Tomorrow, girl,' he promised, smiling at her with a hint of mischief. 'Tonight, I need you . . .'

Patti looked at him doubtfully. She could never trust those dancing dark eyes, the sudden changes of mood. She could never be sure just how much he meant the things he said, the things he did. The light words were entirely in character, of course. He lived and loved for the moment. Tonight, he wanted her and to hell with everything else. Tomorrow, he would be saying much the same things to Jenefer or some other girl.

'Tonight, there's Steve,' she said, very firm. She had to be firm. She wanted so much to slip into the wonderful world of delight in his arms. 'Tonight and always!' That was not true but she had to protect herself from that constant and growing temptation.

'Steve,' he repeated wryly. 'Yes, of course. Do you know, I'd forgotten about him . . .' Which wasn't surprising when she was so responsive, so melting, firing his blood and filling his unaccustomed heart with loving.

'You seem to have forgotten Jenefer, too,' Patti said quietly.

'Do you worry about Jenefer?' he asked, quick, eager with new hope. 'There's no need, Patti. She doesn't mean very much . . .'

'None of us do, Ivor,' she said lightly, her heart swelling with the painful conviction that it was only too true.

Ivor felt an instinctive dislike that she should lump herself with all the women who had meant so little in his life. Before he could protest, declare that she meant a very great deal to him, the music ended on a noisy roll of drums and she slipped from his arms. She turned to Steve and Jenefer, close behind them, and the moment was lost.

When they returned to the table and their drinks, Patti took pains to sit as far from Ivor as possible. He thought she also took pains to show him that a mere physical response she could not help did not affect the way she felt about the man she was going to marry. She sat very close to Steve, smiled on him with loving warmth, listened to his words and laughed at his jokes with as much admiring attentiveness as if they were already married.

Ivor told himself that she obviously loved the man, hard as it was for him to accept. Only a kind of chemistry existed between them. It had sparked him to an awareness of love for the first time in his life. But her heart had been immune because it already belonged to another man.

He was sorry that they could not even be friends. But it was out of the question. He would always want Patti too much to be content with a platonic relationship. And she admitted with an endearing frankness that she found him too sexually attractive for comfort. So he must follow her lead and behave as though they were the merest acquaintances rather than risk sparking that dangerous flame into new and consuming life.

It was just as well that he was going away the next day. Distance would not lessen the way he felt about Patti, of course. But it would give him time to come to terms with the realisation that she would never really belong to him . . .

Patti was thankful that Ivor did not ask her to dance again. She would have had to refuse. Her cheeks still burned when she thought of the way their bodies had fused on the dance floor in full view of anyone who cared to notice. There had been so much intimacy in the way he held her, the way he looked, that she marvelled that the whole of Hartlake did not know that they were past lovers who longed to be lovers again.

It hurt to watch while he danced with Jenefer or Joanne or Daisy or one of the other girls in their party. It hurt that he held each one in a near-embrace, smiled in the way he had smiled at her and probably teased and tempted them just as he had done with her. He was a rake who would never be anything else, Patti told herself with a sigh. Every woman stirred his senses in exactly the same way. Any woman could ease that need and delight him. She must have been mad to think that there had been something special in the way he held her, the way he smiled, the way he looked and spoke. It was all part of his stock in trade as a womaniser!

She and Steve left just before the last waltz. Ivor was dancing with Jenefer but he turned his head to watch as they threaded their way through the tables. Patti raised her hand in a halfwave and smiled at him, trying to hide the pain of loving and longing that a man like Ivor would not welcome from any woman. He did not smile in return. It was an odd fancy, but Patti thought there was a little glow of anger in the dark eyes . . .

Steve kissed her, a little roughly. She seemed a million miles away as they sat in his car, parked in a side street near the Nurses' Home. He must shortly begin the long drive back to Richmond and he was impatient with her lack of response.

'You're not even thinking about me,' he accused.

'Sorry.' Patti was rueful, knowing it to be true. Her thoughts had been with Ivor who would probably be making love to Jenefer that night. She did not want to dwell on the image of that togetherness but it haunted her, filling her with sick dismay and a bitter jealousy.

She tried to smile at Steve, penitent. He came to Hartlake almost every evening, needing to see her and prepared to put up with all the inconvenience of their present relationship until she came to her senses and forgot her foolish and unnecessary pride —which was how he saw things. But the strain was beginning to tell on him, she knew. It was a constant bone of contention that they had no privacy for lovemaking. She could not take him to the flat she shared with her fellow juniors. They could not make love in the communal sitting-room. Steve was frustrated. Patti was relieved, but she did not want to hurt him by making it too obvious.

Now, they were near to saying goodnight in the usual, unsatisfactory manner as they sat in the car in the quiet road, his arm about her shoulders.

He tried to draw her closer. Patti did not mean to

resist but it was involuntary and instinctive. Suddenly she did not even want him to kiss her. Her lips belonged to Ivor. She brushed the tentative hand away from her breast. Her body belonged to Ivor, too. She could not help the way she felt. Steve frowned, angry and suspicious.

'It's late,' she said, a little lamely. 'You won't get to bed until two o'clock even if you leave now!'

He shrugged. 'Do you suppose I shall sleep?' he asked, bitter. 'I think about you too much. You don't seem to realise the hell you're putting me through, Patience. I love you and I'm only human!' He pulled her to him and kissed her with increasing urgency. Patti's hands clenched against his chest but she forced herself to endure that kiss. Steve was not so insensitive that he didn't realise her tension, her reluctance. 'I don't think you want me at all these days!' he exclaimed, releasing her abruptly.

'Not like this . . .' she said carefully, trying to let him down lightly.

'Then come and live at the flat and let's get back to the way it used to be, sweetheart,' he urged, impatient.

Patti laid her hand along his cheek in a caress from the past to soften the blow. 'I'm sorry. I can't,' she said simply. 'It could never be the way it used to be, Steve.' There was no way of saying it that did not hurt him, she knew.

He stared at her, silent. A nerve jumped in his jaw and he moved his face from the touch of her hand as though he could not bear it any longer.

'I'm sorry,' she said again.

'It's Maynard, isn't it?' He was very grim.

Patti's heart jumped. 'What?'

'That man you danced with—Jenefer's boyfriend. You're in love with him. It was written all over you but I tried not to see it. I saw the way you looked, the way you danced with him. Embarrassed the poor devil! No wonder he gave you a wide berth for the rest of the evening!'

The blood drained from her face at the blunt and shocking words. 'Steve!'

'It's true, isn't it? You are in love with him, aren't you?'

'Yes,' she said quietly. 'Yes, I am.' It was almost a relief to say it aloud.

'Well, I'm sorry to say it but he doesn't want you. Take my word for it!'

Patti winced. Steve believed he was speaking the truth. Perhaps he believed he was trying to protect her from making a fool of herself, from getting hurt. It was more likely that he was being deliberately cruel to hit back at her for hurting him.

'I know that,' she said. It was true that Ivor did not want her as she wanted him . . . with all her heart and for ever.

'Then why waste time on someone who doesn't want you when *I* do?' he asked reasonably. 'I'm asking you for the last time, Patience. A man can only swallow his pride for so long, you know. Give up nursing and come to me. I love you and I'll look after you, make you happy, make you forget that Maynard even exists!'

Patti sighed. Steve seemed to find it a simple matter to give his heart and take it back again as it suited him. She could not. Loving Ivor had become a whole new way of life. Loving Ivor had filled her heart and mind with new and wonderful dreams. It would be impossible to forget him or to be happy with Steve or any other man.

That soft sigh, her silence, the dreamy look in her eyes was all the answer he needed. Steve gripped the steering wheel and rested his fair head on his hands, weary and disheartened. He had ruined a perfectly good marriage for her sake. He had hurt Val, disappointed his parents, upset his friends and taken a risk in transferring to the London office in the hope of coaxing Patience back to his arms. But she had changed so much that now he wondered if it would have worked out, anyway. She was no longer the girl who had loved him so much. He might as well have stayed in Lancaster with Val, who really did care about him and would agree to anything that made him happy. This new and difficult Patience was too wilful, too independent, too determined to go her own way without a thought for anyone's feelings but her own. She would end her days as a lonely old maid—or worse if she went on throwing herself at men who did not want her as she had that evening, he thought coldly.

'It isn't any use, is it?' he said with a note of finality. 'No point in seeing each other again . . . ?'

'I don't think so,' she agreed quietly.

She put her hand on his thick hair. There was nothing she could say to him. He would not want to be told that she would always think of him with affection because of the good times. Just now, he probably felt that he loved her still and he was reluctant to admit that they had both changed.

Perhaps Steve did love her as much as he could love anyone. She did not think he was capable of the deep and true and tender caring that was the most precious gift that a woman could have in life. That was how Ivor would love, she felt.

If he ever loved at all . . .

CHAPTER THIRTEEN

PATTI mounted the wide steps of the main entrance to the hospital with her friends, making her way to the day's work on the ward and feeling lighter of heart than she had felt for several days. It seemed that a weight had fallen from her slight shoulders and from her spirits with that final parting with Steve. He had never belonged to her new life at Hartlake. He was just a dear memory from the past.

Now, she was released from that mock engagement, the result of a foolish and impulsive lie. Now, she could concentrate more fully on her work as a nurse—and on the present, she decided firmly. The past was behind her and the future was always unpredictable. Ivor lived for today and its delights, and that philosophy suddenly seemed to make a great deal of sense.

She might feel that her love for him would last for ever. But hadn't she believed that about her feeling for Steve and gradually outgrown it, known it to die? The beautiful dream of tomorrow's happiness could crumble in a moment. Today's reality should be grasped with both hands.

Today, Ivor wanted her. She knew it in her heart and mind and tumultuous body. His arms enfolded her so eagerly. His voice deepened so meaningfully on her name. That little glow burned in his dark eyes when he looked at her. The flame of desire leaped for him just as it did for her, Patti thought exultantly. She would run into his arms and live and love for today—and let destiny take care of tomorrow!

She hurried to the ward, eager to see Ivor. She did not know what she would say to him, but the words would find their own way from her heart. Or the look in her eyes would surely tell him all that she wanted him to know . . .

Ivor had left early that morning for the cottage by the sea in Norfolk. The sea and the bracing air and, hopefully, the sunshine together with familiar surroundings might ease that persistent ache in him, that never-before-felt need for a woman who did not love him.

It would have been marvellous if he could have taken Patti with him and persuaded her during those few days that they were meant to be together until the end of time. It was how he felt about her, what he wanted.

Instead, he went alone. To think of her and long for her and count the hours until he saw her again.

It was not his fault that Jenefer Neal, off duty that weekend, had decided to visit a friend who had married and left nursing and now lived in Norfolk. It was not his fault that she told Marian Foster that she was spending the weekend with a friend in Norfolk and was really looking forward to it or that Marian innocently repeated those remarks to Patti. It was not his fault that Patti, discovering to her disappointment that Ivor was also away, instantly assumed that they were together.

It was all coincidence, but her shattered heart

thought it was planned. *I want you out of my life*, she had said, not meaning it. *Tomorrow*, he had replied lightly, knowing that he would be with Jenefer and much too occupied to give any thought to her. So much for that foolish belief that she could run into his arms and find a welcome!

The staff nurse was obviously much more important to him than she had believed—or than *she* could ever be for all the promise in his eyes, his smile, his lilting voice. He had never meant the way he looked, the way he spoke, the way he held and kissed her, she thought bleakly. It had never been anything more than a game to him. It had become her whole life.

She was not the only one to leap to the wrong conclusion about that coincidental absence of both staff nurse and registrar. Everyone at every turn seemed to be talking about them. Or so it seemed to poor Patti, who could not bear to think of them together, not only making love but enjoying the long days of summer sunshine and possibly laying the foundations for a deeper and permanent relationship.

It was a dreadful weekend on the ward. Several patients were discharged. Others were convalescent and inclined to be irritable, impatient to go home and irked by the hot, golden days of summer that they were missing. New patients were admitted on Sunday, not one emergency among them, and there did not seem to be very much for the ward staff to do apart from routine rounds. At any other time, Patti might have been grateful for a quiet weekend with no Jenefer Neal to carp and criticise and chivvy her. But she desperately needed to be busy . . .

Jenefer returned to the ward on Tuesday morning, glowing from long hours of sunshine for the weather had been unexpectedly good all over the weekend.

She was glowing with more than summer tan, too, for she had met several of Julia's friends and liked one of them in particular who had gone out of his way to make her brief holiday both successful and memorable. She had come back to London with a promise that he would come down to the capital to see her again very soon. It seemed to Jenefer, desired and delighted, that she had at last found the one man who felt as strongly about her as she did about him.

Meeting Patti in the ward corridor, she smiled warmly and with new friendliness, wondering why she had ever disliked the girl so much and feeling a little guilty about having shown it quite so plainly. She remembered with a small, self-mocking smile that the girl's red hair had always irritated her and now she had fallen quite heavily for a man with almost exactly that shade of hair! She was an awful idiot and most unkind to have condemned the cheerful and hard-working and justifiably popular junior for something she really could not help!

'What kind of weekend have you had?' she asked. 'I hope you haven't been too rushed.'

'Very peaceful,' Patti said briefly, forced to walk those few yards along the corridor with the staff nurse.

'Without me?' Jenefer smiled. 'I suppose I have been a bit hard on you over the last few weeks. No hard feelings, I hope?'

'None at all,' Patti said, sick at heart and hating her.

'I've had an absolutely super time! Sun, sea air, good food—and the most gorgeous man to dance attendance! What more could a girl want?' She surveyed her sun-kissed arms with satisfaction. 'Don't you just envy my tan?'

Patti felt like telling her that she looked as if she had spent the entire weekend in bed with her lover, so self-satisfied, so glowing, so deliciously content did she seem. 'You certainly look well,' she assured her politely . . . and escaped into the sluice.

She was sure that the staff nurse knew just how she felt about Ivor and did not care how much she hurt her by gloating about that weekend with him. She had carefully not mentioned his name, of course. She knew very well that there was no need to do so. Everyone at Hartlake knew that they had spent that weekend together by the sea.

Later that morning, Michael Keen followed her along the corridor in his wheelchair, calling her name. Patti turned, smiled. But the smile did not touch her eyes.

'I wish you'd tell me what's wrong,' he said, concerned. He had become very fond of her since he had been admitted to Currie. She was like an older sister, he felt.

'Nothing's wrong,' she assured him for at least the sixth time.

He looked at her with a sceptical eye. 'I know there is, Patti! You've got that look in your eyes. Maureen used to get it when she was miserable and didn't want to say why! Why *do* women always say there's nothing wrong when it's only too obvious that there *is*!'

'Women are very strange animals,' she said as lightly as she could.

He reached for her hand. 'Anything I can do? Tell me!'

Impulsively, she stooped to put an arm about his neck. 'No. But thanks for caring, Mike,' she said warmly and kissed his cheek.

Michael put his arms around her and hugged her and suddenly found that he did not regard her as an older sister, after all. She awakened feelings that he thought had died with the pretty Maureen on that dreadful night.

Patti straightened, sensitive to his mood and vaguely disturbed and very thankful that a senior member of the staff had not seen that little incident. Flirting with doctors was quite bad enough, but no nurse ever allowed a patient to embrace her, attempt to kiss her!

Then she saw Ivor, watching them from the end of the corridor with a flicker of amusement in his dark eyes. Her face flamed. She had not observed the swing of the doors. For once, she had not been immediately aware of him!

'You'd better get back to the ward,' she told Michael, flustered. Michael nodded, turned the wheelchair and began to propel it towards the ward.

Patti was supposed to be on her way to Paterson with a message from Sister Percival. Her heart was pounding and she felt slightly sick, but she meant to walk past Ivor as though he did not exist. She had found her pride and as far as he was concerned, anything she had ever felt for him was dead! She would not love such an incorrigible, incurable rake who amused himself by taking and breaking hearts as though they were toys!

She walked towards him, head high and skirts rustling, refusing to meet his eyes while her face flamed almost as vividly as her hair.

Ivor smiled, heart in his eyes. He had returned earlier than he had intended because there was no ease for him anywhere without her. He was not due on duty until the next day, but he had donned his white coat and come up to the ward in the hope of catching a glimpse of Patti and perhaps snatching a few words with her.

His heart had turned over when he saw her in the corridor, talking to the young patient who was making such excellent progress, mentally as well as physically. He had seen the boy stretch out his hand to her and smiled, rueful. It was just what he ached to do. He had seen her stoop to kiss him on a sudden impulse and he had been filled with warm and tender loving. She was all heart, lovely Patti. No wonder he loved and needed her so very much . . .

'You're encouraging that boy to fall in love with you, girl,' he said lightly, teasing, as she reached him.

Patti's eyes sparked with sudden anger. 'I imagine that's my business, don't you? Not that there's a grain of truth in such a silly remark and I hope that won't be the next thing seized upon by every gossip in the place!'

His smile died abruptly. He was dismayed, disappointed. He had thought of nothing but this moment all the way from Norfolk. It did not seem possible that she could look at him with such cold and contemptuous dislike.

'What did I do, Patti?' he asked quietly, wry.

Her chin tilted. 'I don't give a damn what you did,' she said icily. 'Now or ever . . . !'

Sister's sitting-room, refuge from the bustle of the ward and more often used by anxious relatives than by the energetic Sister Percival, was close and convenient. Ivor caught Patti's wrist in strong fingers, thrust open the door and bundled her unceremoniously into the room.

Indignant, she wrenched her arm away, glaring at him, refusing to recognise what his touch did to her. 'What do you think you're doing?'

'Trying to talk to a rebellious redhead in a flaming temper,' he said dryly.

'I've nothing to say to you!'

He looked down at her, rueful. 'Hating me, is it? There has to be a reason, girl.'

She was stubbornly silent. She crossed to the window that overlooked the hospital garden and stood with her back to him, arms crossed protectively across her breasts in the attempt to keep from trembling. She had suffered from an over-active imagination all that weekend and now, faced with him and remembering only too clearly the satisfaction in Jenefer Neal's eyes and voice and manner, she could think of nothing but them locked in each other's arms. Hurt and raging jealousy and angry despair and more hurt swept over her in successive tides.

'What's happened, Patti?' he asked quietly.

She shook her head.

Ivor heard the little catch of her breath that might have been a sob of distress or temper. He stretched a hand to her shoulder. She jerked away.

'You won't leave this room until you tell me,' he said in dire tones.

Patti turned then, quick. 'Sister won't be too pleased about that!' She saw the twinkle in his dark eyes and looked away quickly before that fatal charm could begin its work. She wondered if he ever took anything seriously. She thought bitterly that he was more curious than concerned at this moment because she was angry with him.

'Sister Percival and I are old friends,' he told her lightly. 'She's a very understanding woman.'

'She won't understand why I'm talking to you in her sitting-room when I'm supposed to be taking a message to Paterson!'

'But you aren't talking to me,' he reminded her, eyes crinkling with warm amusement. 'That's the problem! I need to know why, Patti. I've been away for three days. So it has to be something that happened at the dance—or after it?' he added with sudden, shrewd perception. 'Quarrelled with Steve, is it? The man saw the way we were together and drew his own conclusions, perhaps. Right ones at that, girl!' He turned her with an arm about the slender waist, smiled at her. 'I can't help wanting you, Patti. I guess it shows. I don't blame him for wanting to punch me on the nose. Does he?'

Patti said nothing. She was too busy fighting that look in the dark eyes, that unreliable but very potent meaning in the drawling voice, that magic in the light embrace.

'Don't worry, *cariad*,' he went on gently, reassuring. 'He won't let you go.' He was very concerned that she should be happy, forcing down the leaping need for his own happiness. '*I* wouldn't . . . if you were mine,' he added, very soft, words from the heart.

Patti wondered if she had really heard those words, so quietly spoken. Her heart lurched. Then she told herself with swift, angry pride that it was only words. He was clever with words, smooth, persuasive. But it was just a game to the rakish Ivor Maynard. Only a fool would listen to him and want to believe anything he said!

He had come straight from Jenefer Neal's arms and dared to use that lovely Welsh word to her, to look at her as though she meant all the world to him! He was a devil! Patti's fingers itched to slap that attractive face. He did not care who got hurt as long as he could enjoy his sensual and superficial and cruel game of love!

'I'm not yours,' she said, cold and angry, moving away from him. 'You're the last man in the world I'd want to belong to—and if you were the only man in the world I wouldn't let you touch me again!'

Ivor's brows drew together sharply. He felt as though she had struck him. A physical blow might have been easier to take than that violent blow to the heart. 'It's a lot of hate, Patti,' he said slowly.

'It's the way I feel about you!'

He looked at her for a long moment, saying nothing. Then he walked from the room, white coat billowing behind him.

Sick at heart, very shaken, Patti leaned her hot

forehead against the cool pane of the window. She was trembling all over and her knees felt so weak that she could scarcely stand. She stood by the window for what seemed an eternity, knowing that he would never speak to her again after that outburst.

I hate you, she had thrown at him in angry despair and bitter distrust. No man with an ounce of pride would come back for more after that—and why should he when there were so many Jenefer Neals and there was nothing special about one first-year nurse among the many at Hartlake except for her absurdly conspicuous hair!

Ann Percival came into the room and checked in surprise. 'You aren't supposed to be in here, Nurse,' she said quickly, gently rebuking. 'This is my private room.'

'I'm sorry, Sister,' Patti said lamely, and burst into tears.

Ann stifled a sigh. She had been looking forward to a peaceful cup of tea and the chance to read a letter from an old friend. She was not too pleased to find a pale and weepy junior in her room. But she had dealt with a great many in her time and invariably the tears were caused by an unsatisfactory love affair. She wondered why the first years were so eager to fall in love with the wrong man. Even the promising Nurse Parkin was not proof against that tendency of Hartlake juniors to put romance before their work, it seemed . . .

Patti could not explain those tears to the warm-hearted and sympathetic ward sister who had obviously seen it all before. She could not explain them to herself. She had never cried so brokenly even for the loss of that long-cherished dream of marrying Steve. She was not the type to weep for the might-have-been. She had always felt that there were other compensations in life for lost dreams.

But Ivor was different. Ivor was not just a lovely dream of happy-ever-after that bore little relation to reality. Ivor *was* the reality. Happiness was here and now with Ivor, she knew with sudden clarity as if the tears had swept the pride from her heart and the blindness from her eyes.

Like two halves of a whole, they belonged together. She had always known it. Ivor knew it, too. It was in his touch, his smile, his need of her. He had reached out for her like a man who knew his destiny—and she had been foolishly deaf to all that he said without words.

When had they ever needed words? Loving was silent, a fullness of the heart that could only express itself in touch and look and that warm tidal wave of emotion for which there were no truly adequate words. Nothing could alter or threaten the way they felt about each other. Not a dozen Steves or a hundred Jenefer Neals! Not the foolish past or the doubtful tomorrow! Today was all that mattered, anyway—and today, Ivor wanted her, loved her!

If you were mine . . .

His words echoed in her mind and heart. She could never be any other man's if she lived to be a hundred. She belonged to Ivor, come what may!

She realised that Sister was advising her to wash her face and straighten her unruly cap. 'Then I think you may go off the ward for half an hour,'

Ann Percival said kindly, wondering if the girl had heard a word that she had said to her. 'Some fresh air will probably make you feel much better.'

'Yes, Sister. Thank you, Sister.' Patti's lovely smile was warm with gratitude and bright with new hope.

Glancing through a window as she made her way to the juniors' room after leaving Sister Percival, she caught sight of Ivor. She paused, heart filling and overflowing with love.

He was sitting beneath Sir Henry's statue with hands thrust deep into his trouser pockets and long legs outstretched, dark head thrown back so that the warm sun fell on his face. Even from that height and distance, Patti saw that all the attractive liveliness and lightness of heart was shadowed by his thoughts and she knew that he was as unhappy as herself.

Without pausing to think, she headed for the stairs and went down the several flights as quickly as she could. She hurried across Main Hall, busy as usual, and pushed through the doors into the hospital garden.

The seat he had occupied was empty.

Dismayed, Patti checked and looked around for him. He was not immediately to be seen among the many people who used the garden as a short cut from one part of Hartlake to another. Then she saw him walking away from her, towards the tall gates that led to the street behind the hospital. She had the awful feeling that he really was walking out of her life for ever!

Nurses did not run except in cases of fire,

haemorrhage or cardiac arrest. Patti ran across the lawns as fast as she could to catch him, utterly disregarding that rule, losing her cap on the way and caring nothing for the attention she attracted.

'Ivor!' He did not check his stride. Patti knew he was too preoccupied to hear. Ivor would not ignore a cry from the heart. He was much too caring. 'Ivor!' she called again, gaining on him.

He paused, turned. He stared for a moment—and then he raised an amused eyebrow and the dark eyes began to dance with familiar, enchanting mischief.

Patti reached him, breathless—and he steadied her with a hand on her arm. 'Ivor . . .' she said, hand to her thudding but thankful heart. For there was all she needed to know in his smile, the touch of his hand.

'Patti . . .' he said, teasing. 'There's reckless you are, girl. Matron's Report tomorrow, is it?'

'Tomorrow can take care of itself,' she returned impulsively, smiling at him with love. 'Today is ours!'

'All the todays,' he said softly, heart in his eyes.

She went into the arms that she knew would hold her secure and content for the rest of her life. 'Oh, Ivor,' she said thankfully. 'I do love you!' And she raised her face to be kissed.

'*Cariad* . . .' he murmured, meaning everything that any woman's heart could want to hear—and he kissed her with warmth and tenderness as well as that swift-sparking passion that was so important a part of the love between man and woman that could last longer than any dream.